ANGELA CERRITO

Holiday House / New York

Printed and bound in April 2011 at Maple Vail, York, PA, USA.
www.holidayhouse.com
First Edition
1 3 5 7 9 10 8 6 4 2

Library of Congress Cataloging-in-Publication Data

Cerrito, Angela.
The end of the line / by Angela Cerrito. — 1st ed.
p. cm.
Summary: In the prison-like school that is his last chance, thirteen-year-old Robbie tries to recover from events that brought him there, including his uncle's war injuries and the death of a classmate who may have been his friend.
ISBN 978-0-8234-2287-6 (hardcover)
[1. Reformatories—Fiction. 2. Self-actualization (Psychology)—Fiction. 3. Emotional problems—Fiction. 4. Guilt—Fiction. 5. Uncles—Fiction. 6. Iraq War, 2003—Fiction. 7. Family life—Ohio—Fiction. 8. Ohio—Fiction.] I. Title.
PZ7.C3193End 2011
[Fic]—dc22
2010023475

To Terry

If you kill someone, you are a piece of murdering scum. When I saw his body all twisted and still, I knew...I knew my life was worthless. It didn't matter what Dad said or how hard Mom cried. There was nothing they could do.

It didn't matter that my teachers tried to pretend nothing had changed when I went back to school. "Nice to see you," they cooed. But I could tell by the way their voices got squeaky that they didn't believe a word from their own lips. I could tell by the way their eyes swept over me quick. They looked at my feet or over the top of my head, because they didn't want to look into the eyes of a murderer.

GREAT OAKS ~~SCHOOL~~ PRISON

They call this place Great Oaks School, but it must be a prison. I guess my parents have finally given up on me. They've locked me up. I've been trapped in this room for hours, just me and a school desk with a stack of paper. That's all, except a yellow pencil making a blister on my finger.

A key turns in the lock and the door opens. I'm not surprised to see Mr. Lester, the guy who took my backpack, my belt, my shoes, and even my socks before he pulled my hands behind my back and marched me into this room.

"In the chair," barks Mr. Lester.

I spring up from the floor and leap into the chair. He walks around the desk slowly, like he can't decide what to do next.

"Make a list," he says. "Tell me who you are."

I pick up the pencil and write *Robbie* on the top of my paper and slide it to him.

"What the hell kind of a list is that? Do you know what a list is?"

"Yeah."

"'Yeah' is not a word. Do you know what a list is?"

"Yes."

"Is one word a list?"

"No."

"You can write, can't ya?"

"Yes, sir."

"Good." Mr. Lester picks up my paper and crumples it into a ball. He waves a few papers in front of my face. "Can you count, too?"

"Yes, sir."

He puts a piece of paper on my desk and glares at me. He raises his eyebrows—a sign that he's impatient and I'm screwing up again.

"One," I say.

Mr. Lester thumps another paper on my desk.

"Two."

He keeps slapping papers until I say, "Five."

He holds his hand on top of the last sheet. "You hungry?"

"Yes, sir."

"Well, write me a list. Tell me who you are. Fill up all five of these pages and I'll see about getting you somethin' to eat." He circles around the room keeping his eyes on me every second, and I fill up those pages as fast as I can.

Robert Sander Thompson
Robbie
Robert
Rob
Robbie Thompson
Robbie S. Thompson
R Thompson
Bobby T

Mr. Lester leans over me and swipes my papers to the floor. "I guess you aren't as hungry as I thought." He walks out of the room and closes the door without even a glance in my direction. He locks the door and shakes it. The clank of the metal bolted tight confirms that I am in some sort of jail.

It's about time.

RIVER FALLS

Ms. Lacey didn't even have time to tell us the new kid's name before he dashed to the back of the room, bumped into my chair, and crawled under the desk next to me. Under the desk! Just like Nicholas Spike used to do when he wet his pants in first grade, but this was sixth grade!

"It's time for math! It's time for fun," Ms. Lacey sang. She always sang when we changed from one subject to the next. We all stared at the new kid, so Ms. Lacey sang louder. "It's time for math. It's time for fun," and added a new line, "Robbie, please invite Ryan to come."

I put my book on the middle of his desk and opened it to chapter twelve. The entire classroom was quiet, even the girls. I bent down under the desk and tried to get a good look at the skinny kid. He was curled in a ball with his elbow pointing at me like a weapon. One of his shoes had a hole in the bottom.

"Hi," I said to the back of his shaggy blond head. It smelled like lemons under the desk. "We're going to do math now. Sit in your chair. Okay?"

He didn't move. Didn't make a sound. The math lesson went on without Ryan. Ms. Lacey tried to coax him out for observation circle, music, lunch, and even for recess. Ryan crunched himself into a ball and held onto the leg of the desk like his life depended on it.

Everyone tried to peek into the room at Ryan during recess.

“He’s a freak,” said Dylan.

“Can’t even talk. Bet he’s gonna cry,” said Colin.

“Cryin’ Ryan,” said Tyler. A few of the kids started chanting, “Cryin’ Ryan! Cryin’ Ryan!” In two seconds a crowd pressed against the window for a look. Our principal, Mr. Biggoth—we call him Big Mouth—walked into our room and started waving his arms and blabbing to Ryan. Then he saw us watching and pulled the blinds closed right in our faces.

A minute later, he was tugging Ryan’s arm and pulling him out to the playground. Ryan jerked away and Big Mouth almost lost his balance. As soon as Big Mouth let go, Ryan curled into a ball and leaned against the wall.

Big Mouth bent over him and huffed, “At recess, we play outside. That’s that!” He stomped off.

Every kid on the playground stood around Ryan. A few started to chant. “Cryin’ Ryan! Cryin’ Ryan!”

I went along. “Cry-in! Ry-an! Cry-in! Ry-an!” It’s easy to do what everyone else is doing even when it doesn’t exactly feel right.

Couldn’t they see he wasn’t crying? There was a pink mark around his upper arm where Big Mouth had grabbed him. Kids were calling him a crybaby, and he still *wasn’t* crying.

I looked over at Dylan. He was moving his mouth, but no sound was coming out. I wasn’t the only one who didn’t want to chant.

I grabbed Tyler’s basketball and squatted next to Ryan. “Wanna play?”

He turned his head and spoke under his arm. “I want them to shut up!”

“Go away,” I said. No one moved. “Come on. Just for a minute.”

Tyler held out his hands. “Gimme my ball back.”

I tossed it over his head and watched the guys go after it and start dividing up into teams. Most of the girls stepped back a little bit, but Anna Beth Carter and her giggle girls stayed close.

"Go on," I told her.

"It's a free country."

"Just go, will you?"

"He's not your property, Robbie Thompson."

At least no one was chanting anymore. Anna Beth could be ignored; I'd been ignoring her all my life.

I tapped Ryan on the shoulder. "I kind of suck at basketball," I told him. "I can run fast, get away from the group. But when I get the ball, I miss most of the time."

Ryan didn't say a word.

"If you want to play... it's fun. No one cares if you're good or not. There's nothing to be afraid of."

Ryan looked up at me like he hated me more than anything in the world. His voice was low. "I'm not afraid of anything."

It sounded like a dare.

GREAT OAKS ~~SCHOOL~~ PRISON

I wait. And wait. Brick walls. Steel door. One chair. One desk. One pencil.

Mr. Lester finally comes back. He hands me water in a tiny paper cup. "There's lunch."

I drink it down in one gulp.

"You'll have the same for dinner." He opens the door to go.

"Wait!"

He stops but doesn't turn in my direction.

"Are you locking me in here?"

"Yes."

"Where's my bed?"

Mr. Lester turns, crosses his arms, and stares me down. "You'll get a bed when it's time to sleep," he says.

"You have to feed me."

He smirks. "Really? Why?"

"You just have to—I'm a person."

"I didn't see that on your list," he says, and walks out the door. The door thuds against the frame as he locks it.

A single sheet of paper slides underneath.

RIVER FALLS

After school, Ryan followed me home. I walked fast; Ryan stayed a few steps behind. I crossed the street. He followed. I crossed back. Ryan did, too. So I slowed to let him catch up with me and tried to talk to him.

"Where are you from? Do you like sports? When did you move here? Do you have brothers and sisters?" Ryan didn't answer. I told him, "Kids at school aren't usually like that. You're just...no one knows you yet, that's all." Still he didn't say anything. "Don't wear yourself out talking too much."

"I don't talk too much. I hardly talk at all."

When I got to my subdivision, I didn't turn in. I didn't want Ryan following me right into my house. I walked past Sunny Springs and turned on the back road, trekking all the way around the golf course. It took more than an hour to make it to the front entrance again. Ryan stuck with me.

He turned with me up the path to Sunny Springs subdivision.

"Do you live here, too?"

Ryan didn't say a word. He just followed close. My shadow.

At the gatehouse, old Eddie tipped his head toward Ryan. "This kid with you?" They checked everyone who came and went at Sunny Springs, even kids.

I wanted to say no. But I shrugged and said, "I guess."

My house was quiet. No babies screaming. No two-year-olds

eating paint. No after-school kids blaring the TV. Mom's daycare was just a big empty playroom.

"Robbie, where were you?" said Mom.

"We were just walking." I looked over at Ryan and gave Mom a help-me-get-rid-of-him look.

She didn't help. He followed her into the kitchen, not even a half step behind. He was her shadow now.

"Robbie, come show your friend—"

"He's not my friend."

Mom glared at me.

"I mean," I said, "we just met. He's the new kid, Ryan."

"It's not easy being the new kid." Mom smiled at Ryan and he scooted closer to her. I wanted to ask him why he didn't just crawl under the table.

"Ryan," said Mom, "I'm sorry I can't invite you to dinner, but we're having a family meeting tonight."

I froze. There were only two kinds of family meetings at the Thompson household. They each lasted for one sentence. One kind, the almost good kind: Your father and I would like you to know that you may be having a brother or a sister, but it is too soon to get our hopes up. The other, the very bad kind: Your father and I would like you to know that we're not going to have a baby; it wasn't meant to be.

Mom handed me four plates. I set a plate down at Dad's place and studied Mom. She zipped across the kitchen with choppy steps.

"Who's coming for dinner?"

Mom turned from the counter with a handful of silverware and shook it at me like jingle bells. "Robbie, please. Just set the table."

I set a plate down and moved around the table.

"What'll you eat for dinner?" asked Ryan. I almost dropped the plate. He spoke! He looked down at his feet. "So I'll know for next time."

The phone rang. Mom snatched it before it finished the first ring. "Okay. What time? You have to come tonight."

Mom put the phone in the middle of the table, like it was a vase of flowers, and began dealing the silverware next to the plates. She slapped the forks and spoons down the way Grandma deals cards when she's losing.

"Ryan, let's call your parents. As it turns out, you're welcome to join us for dinner after all." She smiled at him. She gave me a worried look and said, "We'll have our meeting after dinner."

The phone rang again and Mom swooped down on it. "Robbie, get the glasses," she said. She held the phone out from her ear and shook her head. Grandma's fast squeaky voice filled the room. Every once in a while Mom added a few comments. "I know, Mom. . . . Yes, he is your son."

Grandma was probably complaining about Uncle Grant again. She didn't like Christie, Uncle Grant's girlfriend who was sometimes his fiancée. And she hated that he worked as a delivery guy. I set the glasses on the table. Ryan stood at the sink looking at our dish soap like it was the most amazing thing in the world.

Mom said, "We all know what you think of the war." Mom half begged and half warned Grandma, "Don't you dare call the news or even think about trying to phone the president." She set the phone on its base and said, "That woman drives me crazy!"

"What was that all about?" I asked.

Mom turned to Ryan and said, "This phone hasn't stopped ringing long enough for me to call your parents. They must be worried sick."

Ryan dug a crumpled piece of paper from his pocket and handed it to Mom. "My grandparents." Mom took his paper, and as she dialed the phone I headed to my room, alone.

GREAT OAKS ~~SCHOOL~~ PRISON

I make a new list:

I am...
I am a person
I am hungry
I am a boy
I am 13 years old
I am a son, a grandson, a nephew
I am sick of this place
I am angry
I am thirsty
I am skinny
I am a runner
I am a ~~killer~~ murderer

I push the list under the door and lie flat on my belly. I hold my breath and squish myself against the floor, straining to see. Mr. Lester will find my list. He has to.

I can't see anything, not even a sliver of light. I roll onto my back, close my eyes, and imagine Mr. Lester bending down for my paper, reading my list, nodding, smiling. *No, that's not right, Mr. Lester wouldn't smile.*

Please read my list and bring me food.

I can only think about food. Fried chicken, mashed potatoes, biscuits, applesauce, hamburgers, steak, ribs, corn on the cob. My stomach aches. I curl on the cold floor remembering every meal I've ever eaten.

The door finally opens and smacks right against the top of my head. I sit up. Mr. Lester stands with something square and white in his hand.

"I brought you a bologna sandwich," he says, and plops it on my desk.

RIVER FALLS

Mom called us all to the table.

Dad asked, "Where's Grant?"

"Uncle Grant? Really? Uncle Grant's coming?"

She gave a worried look and said, "Robbie, your uncle will talk with you after dinner, after Ryan goes home. Alec, this is Ryan. He lives close, just off Pine Street."

"Hey," said Dad, but Ryan didn't answer, didn't even look up. His eyes were on the food.

Dad loaded up Ryan's plate. As soon as the food landed in front of him, Ryan began to eat—with his hands. He picked up a piece of roast beef covered in gravy and stuffed it down his throat without even chewing. He reached for the mini potatoes, took one in each hand, and ate them in two bites like they were candy.

"What are you doing?" I said. "Use a fork."

"Robbie!" Mom screeched. "Ryan is our guest."

Our guest had gravy hands and emptied his plate the second Dad set food on it. I wanted to tell Mom that *she* invited him, not *me*. But I kept quiet.

After dinner I'll see Uncle Grant, I told myself. At least I had something to look forward to. I didn't eat too much in case Uncle Grant wanted to work out. It wasn't a running day, but sometimes we did sit-ups and push-ups for cross training.

Ryan wolfed down three more plates of food using his hands.

Mom and Dad hardly ate. "Slow down, champ," Dad said. But he said it in a way that sounded like he was impressed with Ryan for eating so much. Mom just kept handing him napkins, pulling mine from beside my plate and reaching across the table to take Dad's from him. After gulping his last bite, Ryan stood up with his gravy hands in front of him.

"Let me get another napkin—or a wet cloth," said Mom.

Ryan zoomed to the kitchen. When he came back he smelled like dish soap. He stood behind the chair with a serious look on his face.

"Thank you," he said, and walked out the front door.

Dad jumped up. "Not so fast, I'll walk you home."

I swung on the porch swing until I heard Uncle Grant's motorbike. Motorcycles, motorbikes, and scooters were not allowed in Sunny Springs. But Uncle Grant worked for a delivery service, and deliveries were always allowed.

"Hey, there's my man," said Uncle Grant. He had a box and a big smile.

He sat next to me and handed over the box. "Something special."

I tore off the wrapping paper and opened the lid. There was an old compass, a few maps, and a list in Uncle Grant's handwriting: underwear, toothpaste, fitness bars, fitness drink mix, granola, black socks, letters, and photos. The last two things had stars next to them. At the very bottom of the page was an e-mail address for Uncle Grant, a new one.

"I don't get it," I told him.

"A selfish gift, really. It's stuff for me. So that you can . . . keep in contact. Because—" Uncle Grant stopped and smiled huge. "I got my orders today. I'm going to the desert."

"The war?!"

"I've been training and waiting. I'm ready."

"You *want* to go?"

"It's not that I want to leave you. Or your ma. Or Christy. Christy's havin' a fit." Christy was always having a fit according to Mom and Grandma. That's probably why she and Grant kept getting engaged one month and unengaged a few months later.

I was used to it, but I liked the unengaged months best because Grant moved out of Christy's and lived in the apartment in our basement.

"Don't go. Tell them no."

"Robbie, I'm going after the bad guys where they live so they won't come here. I'm doing this for you."

"For me?" I tried to sound angry, but I was almost crying.

Uncle Grant draped his arm around me and pushed the porch swing all the way back.

"I wouldn't do it for anyone else," he said, and lifted his feet. The swing zoomed down and swooped up and my heart fell into my stomach.

So this was the family meeting. Then I remembered. "The race. Our race?" He wouldn't miss that. We'd been training for three months.

Uncle Grant shrugged. "I can't help it. I leave in two weeks. You'll still run, right?"

I didn't answer.

Uncle Grant pushed the swing way back again. "You will. I know you will. You'll run it and kick some butt. You e-mail me your time, okay?"

I thought things couldn't get any worse, and then Dad stomped up the steps and pulled me out of the swing. He swooped me onto the railing and hunched over me. He was talking in an angry whisper . . . like he was too angry to yell.

"Robbie, what's this Ryan tells me about gangs at your school? Gangs! And drugs? And guns?! Are you in a gang?"

"Dad," I whined.

He poked me in the chest with his finger.

"Owwww!"

"That didn't hurt," he said. "Tell me."

"Ryan's lying. There isn't a gang at my school. I'm only in

the sixth grade. I heard there are two high school gangs. One for boys and one for girls."

Mom came out. I looped my feet around the rail posts and leaned way back.

"Alec, don't let him fall!"

Dad lifted me to the porch. "Let's get one thing straight. In this family, there are no guns and no fighting."

I looked at Dad. "Why don't you tell that to Uncle Grant?"

GREAT OAKS ~~SCHOOL~~ PRISON

I pull on the door. It's locked tight. I circle the room. One wall of red and gray brick, three walls of rough concrete. There isn't even a window.

Something is really wrong. Mom and Dad have always come with me when I have to change schools. Mom's always determined and hopeful, telling me that the new school will "make a difference." She usually brings loads of cookies or homemade candy, as if a taste of home is the medicine I need to be myself again.

Dad's the one who drives me to the new schools, always steady behind the wheel of the car and awkward in the school hallways. He's quieter and a little bit thinner with each trip.

Where are they? Where is Mr. Lester?

There must be a law about how long a kid can be locked in a room alone. I pound on the door, kick it with my bare feet. After a few painful kicks, I learn that my knees make the loudest noise and suffer the least damage. No matter how much noise I make, no one answers.

I sit on the cold floor and bang my head against the door ten times, twenty times.

"Let me out," I scream.

One desk. One worn wooden chair. I study the chair. It's not as strong as the one I used in that fight at the Superintendent's School for Troubled Youth. It's old, older than the chair I threw out the second-story window at the International School.

I pound my fists on the door with all my might. "Open up! Open up or else!"

Nothing.

I grab the chair and crash it against the door, feeling the vibrations in my hands and up my arms. Smack. Crash. Smack. Crash. Over and over I swing until the chair snaps in two. I take the back of the chair and bash the door, hitting and crunching the wood into small pieces. I reach for the rest of the chair—the seat with two legs attached—and keep smashing. I hit so hard I don't even know what I want to destroy, the door or the chair. With every strike, a few more splinters push their way into my hands. I keep attacking until the chair is nothing but kindling and the dark brown paint on the door is decorated with scrapes and gouges.

I study the design on the door, random splotches and grooves that don't say anything.

I use a sharp piece of wood from the chair to scratch on the door, digging further into the layers of paint until I find silver beneath. The first letter, H, takes me the longest to write, but soon I find a rhythm and the paint peels away at my command.

H E L P

I back up to study my work and decide to add an exclamation point, when the door opens. An old skinny guy with long gray hair wanders into the room. He has a bologna sandwich balanced in the palm of his hand and a paper cup with water on top of that. A big guy in a green jumpsuit blocks the door, his face frozen in a scowl.

The old guy sets the sandwich and water on my desk and shuffles through the bits of wood the way senior citizens look for change at the beach.

"Word to the wise," he says without looking at me.

Why do old people always say stuff like that?

"You best not be playing games when you don't know the rules."

RIVER FALLS

Mom always made excuses for Dad. "Your father just pulled an all-nighter." "Remember, Robbie, Dad hasn't slept. His nerves will be fried." Those were her code words for "Dad might seem nice one moment and turn into Mean Dad for no reason at all."

I heard Mom and Dad talking with Uncle Grant in the kitchen. I snuck down to listen, expecting to hear them talking about Dad unfairly picking on me or Uncle Grant going off to war. But they were talking about Ryan.

Dad was complaining. "He's unnerving, that kid. Didn't say a word most of the way, and then as we got to his house he started talking about kids bringing guns to school. He even said, 'Parents have no idea what kids do behind their backs.' "

They were silent for a moment, probably wondering what I did behind their backs.

Mom said, "When I called the house to ask if he could stay, his grandfather said, 'We don't got much to feed the boy.' And, 'We're much obliged if you feed that boy.' He sounded ancient."

"He was asleep on front porch when we got there. Ryan walked up to him, pushed him on the shoulder and he didn't even open his eyes. Then Ryan told me his grandfather was old and needed his rest."

I snuck back to my room. I wanted Dad to come in and apologize, but I knew he wouldn't. Dad isn't the apologizing type. Dylan's parents were worse. They made him say "Yes, sir" and "Yes, ma'am" when he spoke to them. They have all these weird punishments, like I wasn't allowed to visit for three weeks because I forgot to take my shoes off before walking in the front door. Dylan and his parents had long talks about respect and responsibility. Dad would never talk about an argument, ever.

So it's the perfect time to ask for something I really want.

To: Alec Thompson
From: Robbie Thompson
Subject: My school
Dad,
I don't know about any gangs at our school. Ryan just got to school today and he spent the whole day under his desk (I'm not lying, I swear). So I don't think he really knows anything about gangs.

Maybe he was talking about his old school.

Buckley West used to beat people up, but he's in middle school now.

You could ask Mr. Biggoth. I'm sure he knows everything.

About school, I could use a new digital camera for my insect report. Here's a link for you to check it out: *supercamera*
Robbie

The morning after Ryan's first visit, Mom asked, "Is Ryan in your grade at school? He seems younger, so small and thin."

"He's small, but he's tough. He's not even afraid of Big—Mr. Biggoth."

"I was thinking we should invite Ryan to dinner a few days a week, if his grandparents agree. I'll call there today and ask. Is that okay with you?"

"I guess." I wished I hadn't snuck down and heard about his grandfather. It would have been easier for me to say no. The kids from the daycare could be annoying sometimes. But Ryan was worse. He didn't have anyone who came to pick him up.

GREAT OAKS ~~SCHOOL~~ PRISON

"Up!" The old guy with gray hair leans over me.

"It can't be morning," I say.

He snatches my blanket away. I'm too tired to move. The bed is a gravity force sucking me in. He pulls me by my shoulders until I'm standing, and quickly tugs my bed so it folds in half. I lean against the wall as he rolls my bed out the door.

I sink to the cold floor.

"All clear?" the old guy calls down the hall.

"Clear!" says an unfamiliar voice.

He shuffles over to me and says, "Bathroom. Two minutes."

I groan. "Sleep."

"Son, you gotta get out. I'm not supposed to talk, but you gotta get out, do your business, and get back in two minutes. I have to lock your door."

I didn't even have any business until he mentioned it.

There is a sign on the outside of my door.

Student Number	**101112**
Level	**1**
Tokens	**-241**

Back in my room a desk is waiting for me. On top sit three sharp pencils and a stack of paper. There is no chair.

Make a list. Tell me where you've been.

I take a piece of paper and one of the pencils and sit on the floor. I write:

1. Home. River Falls, Ohio. Where I was born and went to school and was happy until I met Ryan. There isn't a falls or a river in River Falls. I went to Red Brick Elementary.
2. St. Peter's. I went there when Big Mouth (the principal) kicked me out of Red Brick Elementary.
3. Superintendent's School for Troubled Youth in Blue County. Don't even ask how I ended up there.
4. International School of northern Ohio. A boarding school full of foreigners. Mom and Dad thought it would be better for me to live away from home. I liked it so much that I threw a chair out a window, a closed window.
5. St. Christopher's of the Speaking Cross. It's all Spanish. My parents thought I wouldn't get into trouble if I didn't speak the language. They were wrong.
6. This hellhole—Great Oaks School (prison) for murderers!

Mr. Lester doesn't come, so I slide my paper under the door. And wait.

A million minutes later, someone, probably Mr. Lester, slides it back. "40%" is scribbled at the top and red lines are slashed through my words.

1. Home. River Falls, Ohio. ~~Where I was born and went to school and was happy until I met Ryan. There isn't a falls or a river in River Falls. I went to Red Brick Elementary.~~
2. St. Peter's. ~~I went there when Big Mouth (the principal) kicked me out of Red Brick Elementary.~~

3. Superintendent's School for Troubled Youth in Blue County. ~~Don't even ask how I ended up there.~~
4. International School of northern Ohio. ~~A boarding school full of foreigners. Mom and Dad thought it would be better for me to live away from home. I liked it so much that I threw a chair out a window, a closed window.~~
5. St. Christopher's of the Speaking Cross. ~~It's all Spanish. My parents thought I wouldn't get into trouble if I didn't speak the language. They were wrong.~~
6. ~~This hellhole~~—Great Oaks School ~~(prison) for murderers~~!

Mr. Lester wrote, *I didn't ask for an opinion. Lists do not include commentary!* On the back of my paper he scribbled, *Here's a list that may interest you!*

100%	Double portion meal, two side dishes, two fruits, milk, juice, dessert
90-99%	Double portion meal, two side dishes, two fruits, milk, juice
80-89%	Single portion meal, two side dishes, two fruits, milk
70-79%	Single portion meal, one side dish, two fruits, water
60-69%	Single portion meal, one side dish, one fruit, water
50-59%	Single portion meal, one fruit, water
40-49%	Single portion meal and water
<40%	Bread and water

The door wiggles. I hunch over my desk with my pencil ready and wait for Mr. Lester. The old guy comes in. He doesn't say a word or even look at me. He sets a big book and a sheet of paper on my desk. The paper reads: *Write the definitions.* There are only two words on the page—*list* and *commentary*. The book is a dictionary.

I copy the definitions perfectly and slide my work under the door.

Lunch is another bologna sandwich.

I'm going to starve.

RIVER FALLS

At least I finally had someone to walk home with; my real friends all rode the school bus and had so many after-school activities they hardly ever had time to bike to my house. One day I asked Ryan, "Why don't you live with your mom and dad?"

"My mom's in the hospital. As soon as she's better, she's coming for me, and we're going back home."

Ryan pointed across the street. "What's that?"

"Looks like flowers," I said without stopping to really look.

Ryan crossed the street. "Robbie, come here." A pale wooden cross was pushed into the dirt. Bunches of flowers lay around it. On the ground was a picture of a girl with long red curls. "I hate these things," Ryan said. "Don't these idiots know what cemeteries are for?"

I shrugged.

"Did you know her?" Ryan's voice was rough, like he thought I put the flowers there.

"No," I said. "I heard about a girl dying here in a car accident, but that was a long time ago. Last year, I think."

Ryan looked up and down the street. "No one around." He kicked one of the flower bunches and another and another. He even kicked the cross until it broke in half, and stomped on it until it crunched even more.

"What are you doing? Stop!"

Ryan just kept jumping up and down, mushing the flower petals into the ground.

"Stop, someone is going to see you," I said.

He checked the road again and looked down at his destruction. "It's not pretty, but it was the right thing to do."

"It was *not*." I jogged across the street and started home at a fast walk.

Ryan caught up with me. "I hate stuff like that," was all he said.

At my house, a four-year-old boy raced into Ryan's arms. "Hey, Scooter!" Ryan picked him up and swung him around in a circle. Ryan acted like Mom's daycare assistant: telling jokes to the after-school kids, tracing the hands and feet of the toddlers. He had to stay outside of the infant room, Mom's orders. But he constantly stood nearby to check on the babies, like a daycare watchdog. As soon as a baby started to whimper, he'd call out to Mom, "That one's crying! That one's crying!"

Once I saw him walk on his hands from one end of the hallway to the other. The little kids clapped and giggled. "If you acted like this at school, maybe some of the other kids would start to like you," I told him.

Ryan brought his feet down and pushed the hair out of his eyes. "I don't want them to like me," he said. And it must have been the truth, because at school Ryan never said anything or looked anyone in the eye.

The first time Ryan was at the daycare, he pointed to every kid and asked, "What's that one's name?"

"I only know Scooter." I pointed to Scooter across the room, playing with a firetruck.

"All these kids and you only know one name?"

"Scooter's been here since he was a baby. A lot of the others come and go."

"Still, they'd probably like it if you knew their names while they were here."

Even worse, Ryan acted like Uncle Grant's best friend. The second Uncle Grant stepped through the door, Ryan jumped up. "Did you bring your machine guns? Will you let me shoot?"

"No, I don't walk around with a gun, little warrior."

Ryan said, "When I'm old enough I'm going to war, too."

Uncle Grant got all serious when Ryan said stuff like that. "Sorry, kiddo, I'm fighting today so you won't have to in ten years. We're waging a war for peace."

Ryan just said, "Seven years. I'll be old enough in seven years. Maybe there won't be any peace by then."

Uncle Grant asked, "Did Robbie show you our stuff in the basement yet?"

"No!" I leaped over the baby gate, sped down the hall, and stood blocking the door to the basement.

"Come on, Robbie. Ryan'll love it." He took Ryan downstairs. This time I was the one tagging behind.

Ryan noticed all of our medals hanging on the wall. "Wow—are these from the war?"

"I haven't deployed yet, big guy. These are Robbie's medals from racing and a few of mine, too."

Ryan traced his finger along each medal and some of the ribbons.

"The good stuff's in the game room," said Uncle Grant. He stood Ryan by the light switch at the bottom step. "Close your eyes." Uncle Grant turned the lights off before opening the door. "Stand here and don't turn on the lights until we tell you, okay?"

"Okay."

He put an arm around my shoulder and steered me through the dark to the old pool table. "You take this corner and we'll fold it back together. Ready?"

I stepped sideways along the table, lifting the silky cloth high. When the cover hit the floor, Uncle Grant said, "Lights!"

Ryan flipped the light on and rushed forward, his head sweeping back and forth trying to see it all at once.

"Awesome, isn't it?" said Uncle Grant. He bent down and

pushed an extension cord into an outlet. Tiny lights lit up the small buildings, the people began to move, and the water mill started to turn. A fan made the flags blow back and forth over the castle.

Ryan walked super-slow around the pool table.

"What do you call it?" he asked.

"Grantville," said Uncle Grant.

"Robbieland," I said.

Ryan didn't look up. He shook his head. "Needs a better name than that."

Uncle Grant walked with Ryan and pointed out every detail. He lifted up the tarp and explained how all of the switches worked. He picked up a measuring cup, poured water into the well and flipped a switch on the maid's back. She pulled a rope and a tiny bucket came up with water in it. We had worked weeks to get that just right.

Ryan leaned into the middle of our city. He traced his fingers along the castle stones, lifted up the drawbridge, and dipped his fingers in the moat. He was King Kong, capable of destroying Robbieland with a single sweep of the hand, but Uncle Grant didn't tell him to stop.

I pulled out a red disk and set up seven tigers around the edge.

"Merry-go-round?" asked Ryan.

"Even better," I said. I clipped a hoop in front of each tiger. "We're going to make a circus at Robbieland. A tightrope walker, elephants, clowns—"

Uncle Grant interrupted. "Not a circus, Robbie. This is medieval times. There are some performers, but not really a circus."

I snapped the last hoop into place. "Look. We need to get another motor, but when this is set up just right, all of the tigers will jump through the hoops at the same time."

"You could even light the hoops on fire," said Ryan.

Uncle Grant looked up from dripping blue food coloring into the river. "No flames around Grantville, too dangerous."

Fire would be perfect for the tigers, like a real circus.

Uncle Grant walked closer to us and put a hand on my shoulder. "Understood?"

"Understood," I said. Then I remembered that Uncle Grant was leaving in three days. No time to search the junkyards for scrap motors. No time to paint the faces on the performers. No time for the circus. No time for Robbieland.

GREAT OAKS ~~SCHOOL~~ PRISON

Mr. Lester Where are you??? I write in small print in the corner of my paper, tear it off, and slide it under the door. I have only three sheets of paper left. Mr. Lester wasn't around to give me more, not yesterday, not today.

I'm still locked in my room. Alone. For two days.

I make my own lists.

Questions for Mr. Lester:

1. Are you a teacher?
2. Are you a psychologist type?
3. Is Great Oaks really a prison?
4. Do my parents know I'm here?
5. How many days do I have to stay here?
6. Are there other kids here?
7. Can I eat some different food?
8. Can I call my parents?
9. Can they call me?
10. Why not?
11. Why can't I come out of my room?
12. Why isn't my name on the door?
13. Why is my number 101,112?
14. Were there 101,111 kids here before me?
15. Why do I have -241 tokens?
16. What are tokens?

17. Who sent me here?
18. What do I have to do to get out of here?
19. When are you coming back?

What I've done for two days:

1. Breakfasts—two pieces of hard dry toast and two paper cups of water.
2. Lunch—bologna sandwich (two pieces of bread and one piece of meat, no lettuce, no mayo, no mustard, no tomato, nothing) and two paper cups of water.
3. Dinner—same as lunch.
4. Stared at the walls.
5. Talked to myself.
6. Tried to talk to the guy who brings my bed at night.
7. Tried to talk to the guy who takes my bed in the morning.
8. Slid three notes under the door.

The guy with the big nose barges in, rolling my folded bed behind him.

I try again. "Hey." My voice is scratchy from hardly talking. "How's it going? Want me to help?" I rush behind the bed and push. "Is it nighttime? Is it warm outside? What's your name?"

Big Nose doesn't answer. He glances at me a couple of times. He backs out of the room and locks the door. *How do they expect me to survive like this? How do I even know if it is day or night? At least in St. Christopher's I could use the phone if I asked in Spanish.*

I climb up on my bed and jump, screaming at the top of my lungs. "Can I use the phone? ¿Me permite usar el teléfono por favor?" I try to sleep, but it doesn't feel like night. When I drift off, the fighting voices come into my head. The voices always yell loudest when I'm right between awake and asleep.

I hate you!

I hate you more!

I've always hated you!

Ryan's voice, teasing. *Poor Robbie!*

And worst of all, *I'm going to kill you!*

I jump up in a cold sweat. My bed smells moldy. The room feels smaller. I pound on the door. "Can anyone hear me?"

I press my ear to the cold door. I'm almost sure I hear a faint "Shut up!"

I bend down and scream through the keyhole. "Hello?! Did someone say that?"

Nothing.

I can't sleep. The smell of the bed makes me want to vomit—impossible with my always-empty stomach. My feet are frozen, dirty, itchy, and covered with a thick layer of crud. I pull my knees to my chest and tuck my feet under my blanket.

The first day here, I asked Mr. Lester when I could get my shoes and socks back.

"No socks. No shoes," he'd answered.

"Slippers then?"

He'd just laughed.

That was days ago. Mom would freak if she knew I hadn't changed my underwear in four days. Or is it five days?

My body is weak from lack of food. And exercise. The last time I did anything that required strength was swinging the chair at the door. I realize that I can still exercise. By myself. I roll onto my stomach and do push-ups until my arms shake. Then I stand and do lunges, deep knee bends, even a wall sit. I don't have the powerful feeling I get when I run. But my legs and arms already feel different...stronger.

RIVER FALLS

I was playing with the preschool kids with Ryan when the doorbell rang. Mom called, "Robbie, it's Dylan and Tyler."

I finished tracing around a little boy's hand and went to the front door. When I passed Mom in the hallway she said, "You and Ryan can go out and play, but don't invite them in. I have enough kids in here already."

I wanted to tell them to meet me by the garage, but Mom had left the door open and I was too late. They had already seen Ryan.

"What is he doing here?" asked Dylan.

"Check it out, he's walking on his hands," said Tyler.

"Let's just go." I pulled the door shut behind me and walked to the garage for my bike.

Tyler jumped on his bike. "Is Ryan an acrobat?"

"I don't know. He can walk on his hands and he knows how to juggle." I didn't mention that he was teaching me to juggle.

As we coasted down my driveway Dylan asked, "Is Ryan your friend now?"

"He helps my mom with the daycare, that's all," I said.

The day before Uncle Grant left was parent-teacher conference. No school. Our doorbell started ringing at 6:45 as usual. Parents plopped their poopie kids in the playroom and rushed off to work.

"Robbie, can you hold down the fort, just for a second?" Mom begged me.

Patrolling the playroom was worse than going to school. The brats surrounded me, each making a different noise—crying, whining, begging, screaming, and singing. It was like a toddler symphony. I emptied the toy box on the floor and turned the music to maximum volume. An old lady singing *The Itsy Bitsy Spider* drowned out the sound of the one-year-old boy screaming his head off. Sort of.

Three two-year-old girls dug dolls out of the pile of toys and hit each other over the head with them. They didn't cry.

I sat down and stretched my muscles so I'd be ready for a long run with Uncle Grant. Someone grabbed me from behind and I jumped. "Dad, stop. I'm working here."

He handed me a glass of apple juice. "That kid can scream, can't he?"

Dad bent down and plucked a ball out of the pile. He rolled it to the boy. The kid's eyes followed the ball. It bumped his foot and he screamed even louder.

Mom flew into the room with her telephone headset over her head, slid her arm around the kid's waist, and whisked him onto her hip. He shut up immediately.

"Just a second, hon," she said into the phone. She glared at me and Dad and turned down the music. "Really, what were you guys thinking?"

Mom spoke into her mouthpiece again. "No, I think ice sculptures would be overdoing it. This isn't an engagement party or anything." She left and took the kid with her.

Dad and I looked at each other. *Ice sculptures!*

Dad was wearing jeans. "Aren't you going to work?"

"Your mom's my boss today. I'm setting up the backyard for the party."

Mom zipped into the room and bent her head between us. "Robbie, Uncle Grant phoned to say he couldn't run with you today. He's got too much going on." She clicked a button by her ear and said, "I'm back," to her phone before I could even answer.

Dad sat on the floor and scooted his back to the wall.

"Dad, don't you think it's kind of scary, what Uncle Grant is doing?"

"Yes."

A girl with fifty tiny braids dancing around her head marched over and shoved a baby doll and a pink bottle into Dad's lap.

I stretched again. Just because Uncle Grant was going to miss a workout didn't mean that I couldn't run. "Uncle Grant said he wants to go. Isn't he . . . afraid? worried?"

"A lot of things can happen over there, but Grant has been training for this. As long as I've known him, this is something he has really wanted to do."

"Before there even was a war?" Old people are always saying stuff like "before 9/11" or "before the war" even though they are the only ones who can remember that far back.

Dad nodded. "I think so."

"Are you doing what you always wanted? Architecture stuff?"

The girl with the braids came to check on Dad. He popped the bottle into the baby doll's mouth. "Yeah, I am. I like finding out what people want and helping them get the building of their dreams."

Mom set the boy over the baby gate and patted him on the head. He waddled over to the toy pile and sat down in the middle of it.

"What about Mom? What did she always want?"

Dad looked around and gave a laugh. "She always wanted a bunch of children."

The next night, a gamillion people shoved their way into our backyard for Uncle Grant's party. Like every other grown-up party, there were too many things that couldn't be touched, too much disgusting food no one would want to touch, and too many old people. Four guys in red-and-white-striped jackets played music and sang. Hardly anyone danced.

Uncle Grant was surrounded the whole night and Christy never let go of his elbow. We didn't have even a second alone together. Uncle Grant said three things to me all night: "Hey, Sport," "There you are," and "How's it goin'?" He walked right past me before I could answer.

I entertained myself with my new camera. The zoom feature was incredible. I could take a picture of someone three tables away, zoom up on their face and save it. Then I could pull up the face picture and zoom in on their nose. I got some amazing close-ups: the trumpet player's ear with a forest of hair growing out of it, a little boy's runny nose, and even zit pics. Shane, Christy's step-brother, had a face that was a gold mine for pus pictures!

Even with my camera, the party sucked. I was ready to get away from the mosquitoes and the noise, when people started making speeches. People say the dumbest things when they're drooling words into a microphone.

"I know what you're doin' isn't easy. I can imagine," said a lady with a head full of curls and pink claw fingernails. Can she really imagine living in a tent in the desert?

Some guy said, "I've been to war. I'll be there with you." But most people said, "Come back to us, okay?" and "Good luck."

"Good luck" was the dumbest of all. How can anyone say good luck to war? Good luck dodging bombs? Good luck searching for bad guys? Good luck ducking when the bullets come zooming at you? "Good luck" was stupid!

When I was about to fall asleep from hearing everyone say the same thing over and over again, Grandma made her way onstage. She was fussing and carrying on before she even got her hands on the microphone. "I don't believe in this war!" She waited for that to sink in and everyone quieted down. "I believe it is happening, but I don't believe in the leaders that made it happen. I don't believe it has to keep happening."

Mom and Dad glanced at each other. Two tables away, Christy was squeezing Uncle Grant's arm so hard her fingernails were disappearing into his skin. I pulled out my camera and zoomed in on Uncle Grant's face.

Grandma loved an audience. "There is no reason our young boys need to be going over there and getting into a world of hurt! No reason! And girls, too. Young girls. And single mothers. All those kids trying to make do without their parents. All those families, thousands of families..." Grandma made a little coughing noise, almost like she was trying not to cry. She found her voice again. "Hundreds of thousands of soldiers over there. And families here missing them."

Everyone was quiet. Mom nudged Dad toward the stage. But he didn't budge.

Then Grandma started cussing up a storm about the politicians in Washington. A few people clapped and cheered her on. Uncle Grant looked around. He looked like a soldier, his face solid and serious as though he was making a mental note of everyone who was clapping.

If someone is against the war, would Uncle Grant consider them an enemy?

Dad climbed up on the stage and Grandma waved her finger at him. "You just hold your horses, I'm not finished yet."

"Regina, please, it's late," Dad begged. It was funny seeing a great big guy like Dad up against short skinny Grandma. He took one step closer to her and reached his arms out like a dogcatcher reaching for a little mutt.

She waved her finger at him again and Dad didn't step any closer. "One more thing. Even though I don't believe in this war, I believe in my son. That's all I want to say. Thank you." Grandma took a bow and everyone clapped. Uncle Grant's face lit up in a slow smile.

Uncle Grant was walking to his truck when I found him.

"You're leaving? Without saying good-bye?"

"Hey, kiddo. I'll be around early tomorrow on my way to the airport."

In the morning, Uncle Grant came and sat on the edge of my bed. He handed me a white box. "Two weeks until your birthday. This will be the first year I've missed your party." I threw my arms around him and hugged him tight. Uncle Grant sighed. "It sucks to say good-bye." He crushed me with his hug but I didn't care. "I'm actually running behind schedule. Let's just say 'See you later.' "

I wanted to say *I wish you weren't going.* I wanted to say *A year is too long and I wish you'd come back sooner.* I scrunched down in bed. "Good luck."

Uncle Grant stood up. "See you later."

GREAT OAKS ~~SCHOOL~~ PRISON

As soon as the old guy wheels my bed out, I speed to the bathroom, drink water from the faucet and splash some on my face and hair.

Mr. Lester is in my room when I get back. I consider ignoring him, and the desk and papers. But I can't push away this feeling, almost like happiness, about no longer being alone.

"What are you doing here?" I say.

"Interesting question. Read what it says on the paper and get to work." He leans into the corner and crosses his arms.

I bend over the paper (still no chair). *Why are you here?*

I wish I could ask *him* why I'm here, and if my parents know that I am locked up all the time. My stomach growls. "What do you want me to write?"

"The truth."

"Are you a teacher?" I ask.

"No."

"A psychologist type?"

"Not at all."

I knew it. Teachers want answers that are correct and creative. Psychologists want to hear how I feel.

Mr. Lester wants lists. He is a crazy person and he controls my food.

Why are you here?
1. Because I killed a boy
2. I can't control my anger
3. I'm getting more dangerous
4. A normal school can't handle me
5. I need to be punished
6. This is probably the only place that would take me

I can't think of anything else. I hope my list is okay, since everything I wrote is true and there is very little commentary. Mr. Lester glances over it, nods at me, and says, "Okay, seventy percent."

Seventy percent! More food for me!

Lunch is grilled cheese, fries, water and an apple so small and green it is sure to be sour. I roll it in my hands. I remember climbing the apple tree in my backyard and filling my stomach with small green apples. They weren't ripe and made me sick to my stomach. I've hated sour apples since that day.

But not anymore. I chomp into the apple and chew each bite until it turns to slush in my mouth. I eat it all, even the core.

RIVER FALLS

Mr. Big Mouth, the principal, came into our room just as we were sitting down for observation circle. One at a time, we went around the circle making observations. We were supposed to use all of our senses, but most kids just named things they could see. I tried to hear things far away or use my sense of smell.

Tyler said, “I see that it’s sunny outside.”

Anna Beth Carter looked around the room and said, “I notice that the plants by the window are drying out.”

“Very well,” said Ms. Lacey. “You can water them during recess.”

When it was my turn, I said, “I smell lemons.” I always smelled lemons around Ryan.

Ryan was last. No one expected him to talk, because he never had before. But he smiled up at Ms. Lacey and said, “You’re nice.”

Big Mouth pointed to the printouts on the wall and raised his eyebrows at Ms. Lacey. “Care to explain?”

“Science,” said Ms. Lacey, standing up and nodding for us to stand, too.

“Science?” Big Mouth rubbed his chin. “Looks like horoscopes to me.”

“Time to take our seats! Time for learning fun,” sang Ms. Lacey. We moved to our desks keeping our eyes on Big Mouth. “My students aren’t only school smart, they are life smart.”

Ms. Lacey walked over to the Taurus bull and crossed her arms. "It's the zodiac. The students are observing the sky. And composing original stories."

Anna Beth shot up her hand. "I have a story about my sign, Leo the lion." Everyone else looked down. Only Anna Beth would want read a story in front of Big Mouth.

Ryan raised his hand. "I have a story, a star story."

Ms. Lacey smiled at Ryan and waved for him to step forward.

He grabbed his paper and walked to the front of the room. With the paper in front of his face, he started reading and didn't look up once. "The Lone Star. Once there was a king who loved his son. But an evil man killed the king. The son screamed and screamed and screamed. The evil man was the new king. He lived with the queen and had a baby girl. The son cried and cried. The evil one said, 'Stop right now and I mean it.' The boy cried louder. So the new evil king picked up the boy and carried him to the roof of the tower. He threw the boy so hard that the boy never fell back to earth. He kept going up into the sky until he became a star. The queen only saw her son when she looked in the sky. She named her daughter Star, but that's a different story. The End."

Ryan ran back to his seat. I watched him put the paper down. It was blank.

At the end of the day, when Ryan walked with me down the front steps at school, Anna Beth Carter said, "There goes Robbie and his little puppy."

Dylan said, "He's not a puppy. He's Star Boy."

Ryan turned around so fast I thought he was going to start a fight. Dylan sped down the steps until he was only one step away from Ryan. He threw down his backpack and crossed his arms.

Ryan's face was blank, but he had both fists in front of him. A few people called "Fight!" Instantly, there was a crowd.

"Come on, Dylan. Leave him alone," I said.

"Why?"

"Big Mouth will tell your parents." Most of the crowd started to move away, to the parking lot. "If you miss your bus, you'll get grounded again."

Dylan picked up his backpack. "Whatever."

Ryan kept his fists up and his eyes locked on Dylan's back.

"Ryan, let's go, your fans are waiting for you." He knew I meant the daycare kids.

Ryan took a detour on the way home. "I have something really amazing to show you," he said. He led me through the city park, around the fire station and behind Tiny's Pizza. We followed a path through some trees and ended up at an abandoned strip mall I'd never seen before. Ed's Grocer sat at one end with every window boarded up. Small shops lined the sidewalk—a hair and nail place, boring clothes stores and a comic-book store, Big Wiz Books and Collectibles. All closed. I tried to look through the cracks in the wood covering the windows. I couldn't see anything.

"Not that," said Ryan. "Look behind you."

Behind us was an enormous fence surrounding a bunch of construction equipment and a half-torn-up parking lot.

"I found this place my first day in River Falls. They're grinding the parking lot to bits." Ryan pushed his face as far as it would go into the fence. He looked up at the spirals of sharp wire stretched on top. "If only I could get inside."

Inside the fence, the machines sat covered in a blanket of dirt. The blacktop parking lot was crooked and covered with sludge. The machines were cool enough, but we'd have to survive the climb to get close to them. "Do you know the way home from here?"

"Yeah. Howell Street, just off Pine."

"I meant my home. Wait a second—Howell Street?"

Ryan nodded and pointed. "Over there."

"Did anyone ever tell you that there's a haunted house on Howell Street?"

Ryan started to laugh. "You don't believe that crap!"

"It's true. I've seen it. One eleven Howell Street. An old couple lives there. They throw stuff at kids, even in the daytime. But if you go there at night, they'll get you. Kids have disappeared. Really."

Ryan shook his head. "That isn't true."

"They threw bottles at me and Dylan once. I swear it."

"Come on, it's almost time for dinner." Ryan led the way to my house.

GREAT OAKS ~~SCHOOL~~ PRISON

Mr. Lester walks around my desk, around and around. I try not to look at him, because every time I look up he is looking at me. I hear Grandma's advice in my head. "Wear your poker face." Grandma is very serious about cards. A poker face is serious. Never smile. Don't frown. Set your eyes to look far away. No one should be able to tell if you've been dealt a good card or a bad card. A poker face is a blank face.

Mr. Lester slams his hands on top of my desk. "You were right!" he says.

I hold my breath, look far away. He seems crazy enough to hit me.

"You were right!" Mr. Lester says again. He leans his face close to mine. "What have you got to say for yourself?"

"I'm sorry?"

Mr. Lester smiles until his eyebrows fly up into his bushy hair. "You're sorry," he says. "For being right? Don't you even want to know what you were right about?"

I shrug. I'm not sure.

"What does that mean?" Mr. Lester imitates my shrug. "Do you want to know what you were right about?"

"Yes." It is the answer I know he wants to hear.

"Yesterday, you wrote that Great Oaks was probably the only place that would take you. That is absolutely correct!" He points a finger at me. "They call this place *the end of the line.*"

My poker face slips away, but I have a poker mind. My brain is blank. The end of the line. Forever.

Mr. Lester pushes his hair away from his forehead and says, "The question is—now what?" He waves a paper in front of my face and lets it float down to my desk. "Enjoy," he says, and walks out the door.

What do you want?

I study those words a long time. The things I want are too big for one page, too big for a million pages. My stomach aches. My breakfast was bigger than usual. I had orange juice instead of water, and two tangerines with my one hard piece of toast. And jelly, a tiny packet of grape jelly smeared on with my fingers. No knife. Prisoners can't have knives.

Still, I'm hungry—for food and for everything else I can't have.

Once I start writing, I can't stop.

RIVER FALLS

The last day of school and my birthday were on the same day. Before I left for school, Mom said, "Remember to come straight home, tonight's the big party."

After class, Ryan walked around the classroom stuffing blank papers and abandoned pencils and pens into his backpack. My backpack was empty, but my arms were full of a huge stack of library books to return.

Ryan caught up with me when I set my books on the counter. "I have something for you."

He handed me a plastic shopping bag; it was pretty heavy. Inside were four presents wrapped in newspaper.

"Go on, open them."

I started with the biggest one . . . three rocks each about the size of a baseball. Every present was a set of three rocks, all the same size. "Twelve rocks?"

Ryan smiled. "It took me forever to find them. Don't forget the instructions. I wrote it down step by step."

I pulled out a piece of paper: *How to Juggle.*

"Thanks." I put the rocks back into the shopping bag.

"All you need now is practice."

We headed out the door. "Have you ever been to a country club?"

"Is it like a restaurant?"

"I guess, but with tennis courts and a swimming pool, too."

"I've been to a restaurant three times."

"Come to my birthday party tonight."

Ryan had to go home first, so I ran home. The rocks in my backpack drummed against my back with every step.

"Walk on your hands," the kids begged me.

"I can't."

"Tell us a joke." I couldn't remember any.

"I invited Ryan," I told Mom.

She smiled. "Run up to your room and grab a swimsuit in case he doesn't have one."

Ryan showed up right when the last kid left the daycare. Mom shoved a bunch of boxes into the car and we drove to the club, where I found a surprise. An unhappy birthday surprise: Anna Beth Carter.

"Hi, Robbie!" she squealed, flapping her arms and practically flying in the air.

"Mom!" I hollered. "Mom. No girls. I said no girls."

Mom tugged my arm and pulled me to a table in the corner of the room. She sat down, pushed my hair aside and put a hand on each of my shoulders. She peered into my eyes like she used to do when I was three years old and in very big trouble.

"Anna Beth and her mom are just here to decorate. I know it's a party for boys."

I let out a big sigh.

She continued. "But why don't you want Anna Beth to come? She's been invited to all of your other birthday parties."

I wondered how to tell Mom that just because she's friends with someone (Anna Beth's mom) doesn't mean I have to be friends with their kid (Anna Beth). I couldn't tell Mom that girls are crazy people who act like they're from another planet. Girls talk too fast. They ask stupid questions. There was no way I could tell Mom the truth—considering she used to be one.

Instead, I said, "We planned all boys. I want to stick to the plan."

Mom and Anna Beth's mom filled balloons with helium and

tied them to the fence around the pool. Anna Beth, Ryan, and I threw birthday confetti on all of the tables.

Finally, Dylan showed up with a bunch of guys in his mom's van. We all jumped into the water. Every single boy in my class came. The only person missing was Dad.

Anna Beth sat on the edge of the pool with her feet in the water. Ryan walked round and round the pool staring at the water.

We were having so much fun, it was easy to ignore the few guys who called, "Robbie loves Anna Beth." I just dived underwater and swam away from them.

I swam to the edge, close to Mom's table. Anna Beth's mom was with her. I knew it would be impolite to ask when Anna Beth's mom was leaving. So I said, "Where's Dad?"

"Late, as usual, but he'll be here, don't worry."

When Ryan jumped into the pool, he tried to pretend he knew how to swim, but all he could do was dog-paddle. We were racing across the pool and trying to see who could swim the farthest in one breath. Ryan didn't even get his hair wet.

"Tidal wave!" Dylan bounced on the middle diving board. He jumped high in the air and did a belly flop—SMACK! A big wave sloshed over the sides.

A shaky voice floated down from the high dive. "Look out below."

Ryan.

He jumped up and grabbed his knees. Cannonball. He dog-paddled to the edge and climbed the high ladder again. This time he sat on the edge of the diving board and rolled off. Next, he sat on the high board with his back to the water and fell backward.

The lifeguard called, "No sitting on the diving boards!"

Ryan climbed up again. He hung upside down and let himself fall in. No one said anything about his dog paddle after that.

Ryan's stunts were unbelievable. But even more surprising

was how he could talk other kids into doing them, too. "There you go, Noah, that's a great spin, now try to add a flip to it next time." And after five or six tries, Noah could do a spin flip from the middle board.

He even talked me into trying something I thought never I would—the high dive.

"Come on up, the weather's fine," he said. He walked one rung behind me up the ladder. "I'll wait here. No need to do anything fancy, just jump."

I walked out to the end of the high board and looked down.

"Sit down if you have to," he said.

"The lifeguard said no sitting."

"Awww come on, you can swim. It's only water. Take two steps back." I did what he said. "Great, now look straight ahead and take three steps forward."

One. Two. And I was falling through the air. I really jumped from the high dive. Somehow, Ryan made it sound easy. I didn't even look at the other two diving boards after that; I ran, jumped, and even dived from the high board for the rest of the night.

I rode with Dad to take Ryan home. I wanted to point out the haunted house on Howell Street. Dad started to slow down as we neared 111.

"You can let me out here, Mr. Thompson," said Ryan. Dad kept driving.

"Look out your window. We're almost to the haunted house. Right next to—"

Dad pulled into the driveway of 111 Howell Street and got out of the car.

I couldn't speak.

"Great party," said Ryan. He hopped out and followed Dad.

I locked the car and watched them climb onto the porch of the most terrifying house in River Falls. Ryan went inside.

An old guy appeared. I didn't even notice him before he stood up and shook Dad's hand. The old man sat down in a lawn chair on the porch. He was thin as a skeleton, with skin the color of his old undershirt. His arms, neck, and face had a million wrinkles. He looked up and caught me staring at him. I heard a thump and bounced up in my seat.

"Robbie, open the door." Dad pounded on the window.

As soon as Dad got in, I said, "That's the house I told you about. The haunted house on Howell Street, remember? Those old people, that guy. There're . . ." I wanted to say "ghosts," but I couldn't.

Dad backed out of the driveway. "They're Ryan's grand-parents."

GREAT OAKS ~~SCHOOL~~ PRISON

What do you want?

1. I want real breakfasts—pancakes, waffles, syrup, cereal, eggs, sausage, a big jar of honey, and a knife to spread it on my biscuits.
2. I want to have enough food and to know what I'm going to get to eat. I want good food. And junk food. Regular food.
3. I want my stuff back. Clean clothes—my own clothes. Socks and shoes.
4. I want my bed to stay in my room all the time, and my desk, too. I want a chair.
5. I want to take a shower—a hot shower.
6. I want to know what day it is.
7. A calendar
8. A clock
9. Music. CDs. A radio.
10. My TRASHBOX player and all my games
11. A computer with Internet connection
12. I want to call my mom.
13. I want to walk outside.
14. I want to talk to my uncle and my dad.
15. To talk with anyone.
16. I want to play cards with my grandmother.

17. I want to go for a run outside. A long run. I want to run so far that my legs get shaky and every breath stings.

I know there is too much commentary, but I don't want to cross out any words. I slide the list under my door and wait. The worst thing about this place is waiting. No, being tired when I don't have a bed. No, the worst thing about Great Oaks is starving. And not being able to use the bathroom when I want. I suddenly wish I could get my list back. I want to write one more thing: *I want my door unlocked so I can go to the bathroom when I need to.*

Like a normal person.

RIVER FALLS

The night of my birthday party, I kept waking up feeling like I was late or forgetting something. Every time I opened my eyes I thought of Ryan living in a haunted house.

Finally, I remembered my cross training. I got out of bed and started with push-ups. Part of me thought I could skip exercising because I swam for two hours today at my party. *Would it really matter if I missed a few exercises?*

But I knew what Uncle Grant would say. "It's what a runner does when he's not running that makes him a champion." We had a plan. I was going to stick to it, even if Uncle Grant wasn't here to do it with me.

I counted crunches, huffing each number out loud as I sat up. Lunges. They didn't even feel like real exercise, but they were part of the plan.

After exercising, I still couldn't sleep. I remembered the first time I saw 111 Howell Street and Dylan told me about all the children who disappeared there. "They lock kids up in the basement. There might be some trapped in there, waiting to be rescued."

We walked past the front of the house a few times, but the old guy—Ryan's grandfather—sat on the front porch. We walked around the block to the middle of Crabapple Lane and cut through someone's yard to get close to the haunted house. The basement windows were tilted out.

"For air," Dylan whispered in my ear. "They want the children to die slow."

We crawled on our hands and knees from the garage along the gravel driveway until we reached the first basement window, and called down to the children we thought were trapped there. "Can you hear us? Are you alive?"

"What the hell are you boys doin'?" It was the skinny old man and he was waving something at us. We ran full out. Glass shattered behind us.

"He threw a bottle at us!"

"Yeah," said Dylan. "But we could have been captured."

They were just creepy old people. They probably didn't keep kids in their basement.

They let Ryan out every day.

My room seemed to be watching me. I shone my flashlight around to make sure I was alone. The light hit my birthday present from Uncle Grant, still waiting for me to open it. My alarm clock read 2:46.

I shredded the ribbon with my teeth and slid off the paper. I held the flashlight high in one hand and lifted the lid. Deep inside the box was a blur of red and yellow. I turned on the lights and saw my present clearly. With two hands, I pulled it out of the box.

Six perfect tigers. Six thin red hoops. I turned it to look at every tiger. They all had fierce yellow-green eyes and open mouths full of sharp pointy teeth.

I put it on the nightstand, unplugged my clock and plugged it in. When I flipped the switch, each tiger jumped perfectly through his hoop.

It must have taken Uncle Grant forever to finish before he left. I wanted to call him.

To: Grant Reynolds
From: Robbie Thompson
Subject: Thank you
It's the middle of the night, but who cares since I don't have

school anymore? Okay Mom and Dad will care. I'm just
saying THANK YOU for the amazing gift. Robbieland-I mean
Grantville-really will have a circus one day.
Bye
Robbie

Mom woke me up by shoving a phone in my ear. "Robbie, open your eyes. It's Uncle Grant."

He asked about my birthday, but I had other questions.

"Where are you? *How* are you? Are you—okay?"

"I'm in New Jersey. This is the first time they let us use the phone."

"There's a war in New Jersey?"

Uncle Grant laughed. "No, my man. Training. I learned gobs of stuff. Hope I don't have to use it, but it's good to know. Hey, I found out where they're sending me," he said.

I ran downstairs and grabbed the magnet pen off the fridge. Uncle Grant spelled the name of the city. Tikrit. Iraq. Far away. The middle of a war.

I wrote the letters in the center of Mom's Mega Magnet Calendar that covers half the fridge. Everything important was written there.

Uncle Grant talked about training and missing us and going to the desert.

I leaned against the fridge and made a circle around "Tikrit."

"Are you getting your long runs in? Are you ready for the race?"

"I'm doing everything. I even did crunches last night in the middle of the night."

I drew bigger and bigger circles around "Tikrit" until I got to the edge of the Mega Calendar. Tikrit looked smaller in the center of a bull's-eye. Mom begged for the phone.

Uncle Grant said, "You make sure your dad puts it in his planner to drive you to the race. Don't let him forget."

"Dad probably can't come. Grandma's driving me."

"You need a backup plan. Grandma's car can't be trusted. Tell your ma to drive."

"She can't. She has a doctor's appointment. She'll be there by the end of the race." I promised to come up with a backup plan and to e-mail Uncle Grant photos from my birthday party. "Mom needs to talk now," I said. "Good-bye."

"No," said Uncle Grant. "See you later."

I smiled. "See you later." I gave Mom the phone and headed to my room.

Mom managed to take eighty-two pictures of one short party. Some were great: me in the middle of a dive from the high board, Tyler with his head way back blasting water from his mouth, a giant fountain, and Ryan hanging upside down from the diving board by his knees. He looked even skinnier wearing only a bathing suit. I wondered if he would be coming over as much since he wouldn't be following me home from school.

While the photos attached to Uncle Grant's e-mail, I surfed the Internet. I entered the word I'd been staring at since Uncle Grant spelled it: "Tikrit." The search found over 2,000 web pages.

The first few didn't tell me anything. Some old ruins were found there. Some guy was born there. It is located northwest of Baghdad and the weather forecast was "mostly sunny." I looked up "Baghdad." Big mistake. There were a gazillion web pages. The ones I saw were all about the war.

Fourteen people killed. Eighty people injured. Fighting here. Fighting there. Cars exploding everywhere. Five bodies found in front of a warehouse. Twenty corpses found inside.

I couldn't resist clicking on the link. The first thing I saw was a picture of dead bodies lined up on the street. "Gross!"

"What's gross?" Dad stood in my doorway.

"Dead bodies."

"What're you looking at?" Dad stepped into my room.

"I'm reading about where Uncle Grant's going. Tikrit. And Baghdad."

Dad reached over and Xed my Internet page. He pulled up a

chair and talked with me for a hundred hours. About war. About not worrying. About how the Internet isn't the best place to get information.

"Uncle Grant will send us letters. That's the best way to know how he's doing. If something terrible happens in River Falls—a fire, a car accident—it wouldn't make sense for Grant to worry about us, right? We probably won't be anywhere near it. We might not even see it. Understand? Baghdad is an awfully big city. So's Tikrit, I'm sure."

To change the subject I reminded Dad about my race. "This is the longest race I've ever run. You have to come; you've never seen me race." I stopped so it wouldn't sound like I was whining. Dad didn't tolerate whining. "Besides, Uncle Grant's not here. I've never run alone before."

Dad recited his favorite lecture: He can't promise anything and it is the nature of his job to put in long hours, unscheduled hours. I know this lecture by heart. Late nights. Missing sleep. Important details. And his favorite line, "One miscalculation, one mistake, a whole building could fall down."

He talked for so long, I was glad when Mom called, "Robbie! Ryan's here."

Ryan sprinted up the stairs and almost crashed into me as I walked out of my room. "Did I get here in time for breakfast?"

GREAT OAKS ~~SCHOOL~~ PRISON

Plopped in the center of my toast, my jelly looks like a rectangular purple mountain. But when I spread it with my pinky (still no knife) it doesn't cover even half the toast. I sit on the floor holding my toast and wonder if my last list was good enough.

I need something new to eat. Every lunch and every dinner is grilled cheese, sour apple, french fries, and a packet of ketchup—good for the fries and the grilled cheese, but yuck with a sour apple.

Mr. Lester walks in carrying a chair. He sits down at my desk and smooths out a piece of paper. From where I sit on the floor he looks enormous.

He flashes me a big show-your-teeth smile and says, "That was some list you wrote. Some things I can do. Some things I can't. Number one, food. You know the rules. You have to earn the food. I can't make you any promises there. A knife? Were you joking? Come on!"

I pull my knees close to my chest, sliding my dirty feet on the cold floor. I am locked in a prison where I'm not allowed to wear socks; did I really ask for a knife?

"Number two, clean clothes. No problem. Actually, I'm glad you asked, and the shower, too. Think it's easy for me being in here with you? You stink. But no socks or shoes. Not allowed." My Lester looks down to make sure I'm listening. "What else?" He looks over the list like he hasn't even seen it before. I wrote it yesterday, a whole day ago.

"Bed, desk, okay. We can try it." He looks over at me again. "Try it. I said *try* it. If you get rough, start tearing things up, out they come. You get nothing. Understand?"

I nod. "Yes, sir."

"No, I'm not sure you do understand. Have you ever noticed the sign outside of your door? The one that lists your token accumulation?"

"Yes, sir."

"You owe a debt of tokens to this school. You destroyed one of our chairs. You've vandalized one of our doors. You are responsible for your actions here."

"I'll... I won't..."

Mr. Lester ignores me and says, "A calendar. A clock. We'll try it." He peers over the top of the paper. "Music? Computer? Games? Where exactly do you think you are, Robbie? Disneyland?"

"No. You asked what I wanted and... I'm sitting here all day doing nothing. I could be... productive or something."

"Productive? With your little gamie games?"

I swallow hard and look down at my feet.

Mr. Lester clears his throat. "No music. No computer. No video games. None of that."

I didn't even realize I was holding my breath until I let it out.

Mr. Lester raises his voice. "Want to know why?"

I shrug. *What does it matter?*

"Do you want to know why?"

"Yes." I have figured out that Mr. Lester repeats himself when he thinks I've given the wrong answer.

"Because I need you here, that's why. No escaping into la-la land with all that electronic crap. Now, what else?" Mr. Lester talks with a baby voice. He sounds like a six-year old on the playground. "I want to call my mommy. I want my mommy. Do you want your mommy, Robbie? Do you?"

I shrug. I want to crawl under my desk. I want to punch Mr. Lester right smack in the center of his face.

"Well, do you? Do you want your mom?"

I stand; my hands quickly tighten into fists. I need these fists, not to fight but for something to hold on to. "Yes," I say. "It's on my list, isn't it? Of course I want to call my mom. You asked me what I wanted!"

"Well, you can't do that. Not now. Same with talking to your dad, your uncle, or playing cards with Granny. Not for a while, anyway."

How long is a while? How long have I been locked up in this place?

"Hmmmm, one more thing. 'I want to talk with anyone.' We can make that work."

There *are* other kids here! Finally, I'll get to talk someone who probably hates it here as much as I do.

Mr. Lester pulls a deck of cards out of his pocket and starts to shuffle. "Talk with me."

RIVER FALLS

Ryan practically ran all the way to the construction site. I heard the noise before I saw it. The machines were back at work crunching up the old parking lot. Ryan sat on the grass in front of the gate, crossed his legs, and put his chin in his hand like he was watching a great movie. I sat down next to him. "Watch carefully," he said.

There wasn't a lot to see: machines jerking around, a big cloud of dirt, and a pile of black parking lot chunks.

"What am I supposed to be looking for?"

"Everything. How they move the levers to make 'em work. How they lock up. Where they put the key. If there's more than one way to get into this place."

What normal kid wants to sit in the sun all day watching a bunch of old guys work? "Let's see if my mom will drive us to Dylan's," I said and then remembered Dylan was leaving for space camp. "Or Tyler's."

"No."

"Let's go to my house and watch a movie."

"No. We gotta figure out how to get in there."

No way was I going to let Ryan get me in trouble. "I gotta do my run. My race is in three days."

"Races are stupid."

I jogged home and ran a three-mile figure-eight around Sunny Springs. My legs flew, my breathing was even, the running was easy. I grabbed a new water bottle and an apple from the fridge and walked downtown to cool off. Ryan was still sitting at the construction site.

He ran over to me. "I have an idea. Watch this." He strolled right up inside the gate like he owned the place. A big guy blocked his path. He had two big black "T's" on his yellow hat. "Where you think you're goin'?"

"I'm goin' to see my dad," said Ryan. He walked around the guy.

The construction man grabbed Ryan by the back of his shirt. "You're not doin' no such thing. Which one of 'em's your pa?"

Ryan pointed to the bulldozer, his favorite machine. When T.T. turned his head, Ryan shook free and sprinted. T.T. took off after him. Someone sounded a loud whistle.

The machines stopped moving and crunching. The men stood up for a good look. T.T. caught Ryan by his shoulder and tugged him near a blue pickup truck. Keeping one hand on Ryan, he opened the door of the truck, reached in and grabbed something. His voice called out over a speaker. "Which one of you has a boy named..."—his voice faded softer—"What's your name, kid?"

"Ryan." Ryan's voice broadcast through the construction site. "My name's Ryan."

"Who's got a kid named Ryan?" T.T. asked again.

None of the men moved. A few minutes later, Ryan ran toward me. T.T. chased him and hollered, "Get out and stay out! This ain't no place for little boys! I'll call the police! Don't think I won't!"

Ryan's smile was so big it looked like it might fall off his face.

"Did you see me? Did you see me in there? Did you hear my voice? Wasn't that great?"

I backed out of the sun to one of the benches outside the closed strip mall. Ryan followed me and leaned against the store so he could look out at the construction site.

"I thought one of the men might be... you know."

"My dad?" Ryan laughed. "You actually believed me? That's hilarious!"

I didn't think it was so hilarious. Obviously T.T. thought it was possible or he wouldn't have stopped everyone's work to ask.

"If my dad was there, he'd have come over to me. He'd take me around, show me everything. That's the kind of dad he was, involved. But he's dead." Ryan's voice was so calm. Like he'd just said, "My dad's got brown eyes." Or something like that.

"Dead?"

"Yeah. He worked in a dangerous profession. Selling drugs."

"Selling drugs?"

Ryan was still out of breath and seemed happy from his run into the construction area. "It's more dangerous than you think. Fifty percent of drug dealers get killed on the job. Even more get locked up."

I peeled the blistered paint off the bench and threw it on the ground. I didn't actually believe Ryan at all.

GREAT OAKS ~~SCHOOL~~ PRISON

Mr. Lester bends the cards back and lets them flip into his hand. "So, what're we playin'?"

Mr. Lester says he doesn't know poker, gin rummy, regular rummy, hearts, or even crazy eights. He suggests go fish or war.

I pick war.

He deals the deck out and flips his first card, a jack. "Well, Robbie, what is it that you want to talk about?"

"Nothing." I flip a two and he pushes it to his side of the table.

"It was on your list, 'Talk to anyone.' What do you want to talk about?"

"Are there other kids here?"

"Yes."

"Do my parents know I'm here?"

"Of course."

"Do they know... what it's like here?"

Mr. Lester taps his card on the deck. "Probably not," he says. "We focus on results. Desperate parents want to know about our successes, how we turn kids around. We don't actually spend a lot of time telling them *how* we do it."

"How long are you going to keep me here?"

"That's up to you." Mr. Lester leans forward and looks me in the eye.

I look away. Sure, it's up to me. That's what all grown-ups say.

"Up to me? Nothing is up to me. If it were up to me, I'd be home now!"

"Home? I don't think so. Home wasn't even on your list."

I think about that awhile as we flip and scoop up the cards. I didn't write "I want to go home." But I forgot stuff. I forgot to mention the bathroom. That doesn't mean I don't want to go there.

I show a nine and wait for Mr. Lester's card. "I want to go home," I whisper.

"I'm glad to hear that." Mr. Lester turns over a three. "It's something to work toward."

I add the cards to my stack and Mr. Lester stands. He sticks his head out the door and calls, "Earl."

The old guy with long gray hair jogs up to my door. Mr. Lester says, "Take Robbie to the shower."

I follow Earl out the door, but before I go down the hall with him I turn to Mr. Lester. "About the list, what was my score?"

"It was a list of what you wanted. How can any answer be wrong?" he says. "One hundred percent."

One hundred percent! I smile. I want to jump up and down like a little kid. Finally, I am going to get more food!

Earl reaches the end of the hall and unlocks a room the size of a closet. "Shower," he says. "Three minutes."

RIVER FALLS

I walked to Grandma's early on race day. The radio was blaring and I could smell smoke from her kitchen as soon as I stepped inside. Uncle Grant reminded her every race not to cook us breakfast. "A piece of bread and a piece of fruit; that's all we need!" But Grandma said she couldn't help cooking on special occasions.

She dropped her spatula into the pan of browning eggs and ran to hug me.

"Are you burning something?"

"Breakfast." Grandma smiled like I'd given her a compliment. "It's all ready."

Before Grandma finished serving herself, a car honked outside. I peered out the window. Mr. Peters! Mr. Peters is one of those old guys who wear a white shirt and half a bottle of cologne wherever they go. When I first met him I called him Perfume Peters, but I shortened it to Stinky Pete.

Grandma opened the door and waved. "Our chariot has arrived."

"I can't get in the car with him. I won't be able to breathe."

Grandma was walking around the kitchen shoving stuff into her purse. "Yeah, that's Petey, easy on the eyes but hard on the sniffer. Crack a window, you're young and strong."

Mr. Peters jumped out of the car and opened the back door for me. "There's the star of the show, the Olympian."

I stopped and begged Grandma. "Why can't you drive? Your car is here." Grandma's car was always in and out of the shop.

Grandma bent over to laugh, or maybe she was just taking one last big breath before getting into the stinkmobile. "The Jag is here, all right, but it won't start."

Stinky Pete pushed his nose so close to my face I could see hundreds of nose hairs. That would have made a great photo. I tried to hold my breath and dash inside the car, but Stinky Pete managed to slug my shoulder. It hurt a little and I inhaled. Big mistake.

I opened my window all the way. If Uncle Grant were here, he'd be driving and I would be able to breathe. I thought back to our first race. It was only a mile. We ran together every step of the way. At the finish line I was covered with sweat, out of breath, and my calves felt like they were twisted inside out. Uncle Grant tossed me an orange section and motioned me over to a table that advertised another race.

I shook my head. "It's five kilometers, no way."

"Aw, come on," he said, signing his name. "If you can run one mile, you can run three."

And we did. One mile. Three miles (or 3.1 miles, to be exact). Then five miles. And we started training for this 10K. "If you can run five miles, you can run 6.2." According to Uncle Grant, if I can run one step, I can run a million miles.

Thinking of him made me feel more alone.

At the race, I did everything on my own: registered, pinned my number onto my shirt, stretched out, and jogged to warm up. Standing in a crowd of people you don't know feels a little like being in a cage. You can move only so far in each direction. Everyone else was older, bigger, stronger. I closed my eyes and tried to remember what Uncle Grant said before every race. "We're not racing against them. The race is with the clock."

I said my goal aloud quietly: "I will run this entire race." Somewhere there was a little voice telling me that I wouldn't be able to do it. *You're just a kid. This is a long race.*

The horn sounded and the people in front started to move. The crowd wasn't pushing in on me. Running felt like being let out of a cage. I zigzagged through gaps between people and fell in behind a guy wearing purple running shorts and a red tank top. I stayed with him up the hill and all the way to the sharp turn at the 5K mark. Someone held a big sign that read: You're halfway there!

There were people on the side of the road cheering. Purple Pants started to pull away. I wanted to catch him but my legs wouldn't go faster. I remembered Uncle Grant's advice: "You're not racing against him."

I slowed down. Without Uncle Grant there to help me set the pace, I had started the race too strong. I slowed down so much that an old wrinkled woman speedwalker started to pass me. When you pass someone in a race you have a split second to decide what to do. You can ignore them and pull ahead, nod or grunt and pull ahead, or match their pace and talk. Wrinkle Woman decided to talk. Her fast walking matched my slow running perfectly.

She droned on and on about her children, her grandchildren, and her husbands. I nodded and grunted and tried to keep my legs going as fast as hers.

I couldn't wimp out to an old granny. *I will run this race. I will not walk, not one step.* I focused on the finish line. Grandma would be there, and Stinky Pete and mom. *Would Dad make it this time?*

"A penny for your thoughts?" Wrinkle Woman asked me.

"The—finish," I huffed.

I was actually thinking about Dad. Last time when he didn't show up, I wouldn't tell him about the race. "What's it to you, you weren't there?" I'd asked.

He didn't apologize. Instead he said, "Robbie, if you like to run, run. Don't do it for me, do it for yourself."

Wrinkle Woman said that her husband and her two exes would mob her at the finish line. "I might just keep going!" She smiled. We ran past the nine-kilometer mark and she said, "I'm gonna go for it now." Wrinkle Woman bent side to side as she moved ahead. Her legs whipped around her and her hands flew up high. I didn't try to move my legs faster; I just stretched out my stride. It tightened the gap between me and the granny. I needed a burst of speed to beat her. I kicked my knees out, took short fast breaths, and swung my elbows. I punched the sky. Instead of aiming for the granny, I focused past her, past the finish line, and leaned forward. I ran with all my might.

We tied.

A guy with glasses was waving everyone to one side. I followed along. A tall guy put a medal around my neck. Just then, I saw Mom and Grandma jumping up and down. Stinky Pete was with them. Ryan, too. Not Dad.

I walked to the fence and got a high five from each of them, Ryan first, Stinky Pete (I punched him on the shoulder), Grandma, and Mom.

"Cool medal," said Ryan, reaching over the fence to touch it.

I followed the maze of runners to the water table. Beside the drink stand was a table advertising another race—another 10K. The race was for all ages and in River Falls. I put my name on the list to run. Uncle Grant would have been proud.

GREAT OAKS ~~SCHOOL~~ PRISON

I come back from the shower to find a desk in my room as usual, but my bed is also here and next to it sits a small round table holding a tiny plastic clock and a paper calendar. The calendar has a page for every day, all the way back to January first. I flip back and forth trying to count how many days I've been at Great Oaks School.

Mr. Lester steps in and I ask him, "What day is it today?"

"Friday."

"Which Friday?"

Mr. Lester smiles big. "Friday the thirteenth."

I count the pages on the calendar. Wasted days. Wasted hours. Wasted minutes. And how many more to go?

Sure, I've just had my first shower in twelve days. Finally, I'm wearing a pair of clean underwear. It isn't enough. Nothing at Great Oaks will ever be enough. I hold the calendar in my hands. The clock tick-tocks beside me. I need more.

Mr. Lester waves an arm at me and points to the door. "You ready to go?"

I almost say, "Where?" but stop myself. It doesn't matter. I'm ready. Anywhere is better than this room. I point to my feet. "Aren't we forgetting something?"

"What?"

I suppose it is easy for him to forget about shoes and socks since he is allowed to wear them. "My feet," I say.

Mr. Lester unlocks a small room at the end of the hall next to the showers. It's filled with sheets, blankets, and pillows. He tosses me something that feels like a packet of tissues.

"You can wear those, but they'll laugh at you. Don't say I didn't warn you."

I don't care who laughs. My feet are freezing. I open the packet and find two blue plastic slippers. They're kinda cool, actually, like surgeons or astronauts wear. I slip them on and follow Mr. Lester around the corner. We climb up five flights of stairs. My plastic slippers wrinkle and crunch on every step.

At the top of the stairs, Mr. Lester opens a swinging door and we enter a long white hallway. Unlike on my floor, most of the doors are open, music is playing, and people are talking. Far at the other end of the hallway people are walking around. Mr. Lester steps into the first room. "Come in here."

Three guys are standing across the room by a window. A real window! When they see Mr. Lester, they run to their chairs. A tall, skinny kid with dark skin is the first to see me. He says, "Firecracker."

The other two guys look up. One has greasy red hair, the other is bald and covered with tattoos. "Holy firecracker!" says the tattoo guy.

"Heck," says the other.

Mr. Lester holds up his hands. "Guys, this is Robbie."

Tattoo coughs. "Don't play me. This your kid, right? This 'bring your kid to work with Pops day,' right?"

Mr. Lester shakes his head.

They think I'm his son? Gross!

"What's he doin' here then?" Tattoo asks.

Mr. Lester sits down and waves me to the seat next to him. "I think you three should introduce yourselves to Robbie. We can all rediscover why we are here."

I look down at my feet and walk to the chair. They all notice my plastic slippers at the exact same time. They laugh, just like Mr. Lester said they would.

"Vincent." Mr. Lester looks at the guy with the tattoos.

"Yo, Robbie. Hey," he says, trying to hold back another laugh. "Mr. Lester calls me Vincent. But I'm 76 to the guys back home. Call me 76 and we'll be straight."

"Nelson," says Mr. Lester.

The redhead stands up and bows. He actually bows like he's a magician or something. "The amazing Nelson at your service," he says in a high, squeaky voice. Maybe he is younger than he looks.

Mr. Lester nods to the last guy. "Curtis?"

Curtis has faraway eyes and a mouth that seems almost ready to smile, but never does. He tilts his head to me. "They call me Big 'cause I got a boy named Junior. My father raised me to be a proud black man and I intend to do the same for Junior." Big looks down at my feet. He says, "Firecracker," in a soft voice.

"Now tell Robbie why you're here," says Mr. Lester.

76 says, "76 is the times I got away with it. I'm here for the two that I didn't. Attempted armed robbery and armed robbery."

Nelson stands, bows again, and says, "Once I was a young business entrepreneur. Now I'm an ex-hacker stuck in here."

Big just shrugs. "Case of mistaken identity. Happens all the time."

Mr. Lester turns to me. "Robbie?"

76 laughs. "He musta been jaywalking!"

Nelson says, "Serial jaywalker with bad fashion sense."

76 says, "No, really. Here's the firecracker. Maybe he pulled a squirt gun on someone and tried to hold up a bank."

Nelson comes back with, "Out past curfew one too many times."

Big defends me. "Coulda been mistaken identity. Happened to me."

76 asks, "So what was it, little firecracker? What are you in for?"

"Murder," I say.

They're quiet, but not for long. Big whistles long and low. 76 and Nelson start with the "firecrackers" again. "You some kinda freak, kid?" asks 76. "You one of them little punks that thinks it's cool to go shoot up a buncha kids in school?"

I don't want to talk to these jerks. They have nothing to do with me. I walk to the door. Mr. Lester's voice reins me in. "Robbie, you said you wanted this. You said you were ready to talk. Come back, sit down and join the group, or we start back at square one."

Square one, I know, is an empty room, dirty clothes, and bologna sandwiches.

I slide my plastic feet around. I walk to the back of my chair, look each of them in the eye, and ask, "Why are you saying 'firecracker'?"

"Mr. Lester don't let us swear," 76 says. "We have to say something."

"If we swear," adds Nelson. "Mr. Lester, he..."

"Explodes," says Big.

"So we just say 'firecracker.'" 76 smiles like he's just explained an easy math problem to me. "Go on, say it. Say 'firecracker,'" says 76.

I grip the back of my chair. Mr. Lester clears his throat.

"Yes, indulge," says Nelson. "Give it a try."

"Don't let them pressure you, Robbie," says Mr. Lester. "There is no reason for you to say 'firecracker.'"

Big gives me a lopsided grin, daring me to disobey Mr. Lester. Everyone's quiet. Big's chair creaks as he leans to the side. Nelson is in constant motion, tapping his bare feet against the cold floor.

I feel stuck, like a tug-of-war rope between Mr. Lester and three teenage guys that I don't even like. But here is better than downstairs, so I sit down slowly. "I'm here. But I'm not saying anything."

RIVER FALLS

To: Robbie Thompson
From: Grant Reynolds
Subject: Hey there
How was the race? Wish I could have been there. I'm in a great place with a really cool bunch of people. The sunsets here are the most beautiful thing I've ever seen. Life is good.
See you later!
Uncle Grant

Ryan stood, covered in dust, kicking our door. He held out his shirt piled high with dirty rocks. I was sure Mom would make him leave them outside, but when he asked to wash them in our sink, she just said, "Okay, wash the rocks. Maybe your hands will get clean in the process." I followed Ryan into our downstairs bathroom.

"They kicked me out again today," Ryan said. He was using one of Mom's pink washcloths and gobs of hand soap to clean the small stones. He scrubbed a handful of rocks, rinsed each one, and sorted them into piles. "There is only one choice. We're going to have to go there at night."

"No way."

"Why not?"

"I don't know about your vampire grandparents, but my mom and dad won't let me wander around town at night."

Ryan dried his hands and then smeared a long streak of soap on the inside of his arm and sniffed it. He draped the soapy arm over my shoulders and pulled me into the kitchen—it was almost lunchtime.

"If it's only your parents you're worried about, no problem."

Ryan shoved his turkey sandwich down his throat and smiled up at Mom. "Mrs. Thompson, may Robbie please come to my house and spend the night tonight?"

I choked. I coughed and couldn't catch my breath. I could breathe in, but not out. A crust or something was stuck in my throat. I pounded on the table and looked up at Mom for help.

Mom ran behind me and squeezed my stomach. She actually lifted me in the air.

Something opened up in my lungs and I could breathe. "Stop! Stop!" I bent over to catch my breath, long, deep, perfect, air-filled breaths.

"Are you okay?" Mom rubbed my back.

"Yeah. I—"

"So can he?" Ryan asked.

Even though breathing had felt so good for those few seconds, I held my breath. I did not want to spend the night at 111 Howell Street.

"I don't think that's such a good idea."

Yay Mom!

Ryan looked up at Mom with sad eyes. "What if I stayed here?"

Mom glanced at me like she was trying to read my mind. I just shrugged, but I was actually hoping she'd let him. I'd never had anyone spend the night before. "If it's fine with your grandparents, we should be able to fit one more kid around here for one night," she said. Mom patted my back again.

Ryan wore a baggy T-shirt and shorts instead of pajamas, and he didn't even bring a toothbrush. He squeezed a long line of toothpaste onto his finger instead.

Ryan picked up an old picture of me and Dylan in a frame that said: Best Friends.

"I never saw this before," he said.

"My mom is always making stuff like that."

I wanted to sleep in Uncle Grant's apartment in our basement, but Mom had pulled an extra mattress from the guest room and put it on the floor of my room.

"Help me move this." Ryan struggled, holding one end of the mattress. I pushed with him until we had it in front of the desk. Ryan climbed on top of my desk, put his arms out, and jumped. He landed, giggled like a five-year-old, and rolled off the other side.

We jumped and flopped onto the mattress. Every so often Mom's voice called from downstairs for us to "calm down," "be quiet," or "settle in and go to sleep." Ryan invented dozens of ways to jump from the desk—landing on his knees, twirling in the air, and my favorite, free fall. I stood on my desk with my back to the mattress and very slowly leaned backward...free fall. We didn't stop until Mom appeared at the door. "What are you boys doing?"

Ryan sat on my desk with a plop and looked at me.

"Nothing, Mom."

Mom looked from Ryan to the big mattress on the floor. She walked over to Ryan and put her hands on his shoulders. "Don't make me regret letting you stay overnight, okay?"

"I won't."

When we were both in bed and Mom was downstairs, Ryan said, "I think we fooled her."

"No, we didn't."

"Is Dylan your best friend?"

He was thinking about the picture Mom made. "I don't know."

Ryan sat up in bed. "Tell me something, something that no one else knows about you."

"Everyone knows everything."

"No, they don't. Tell me something that Dylan and Tyler don't know."

It took me only a second. I went to my bookshelf and pulled out my space book. Tucked behind it was a small photo album, the kind that holds one photo per page. I switched on the desk light and sat next to Ryan. I whispered, "This was the only time I ever told a really big lie."

GREAT OAKS ~~SCHOOL~~ PRISON

At any normal school, weekends mean freedom. At Great Oaks, it is the opposite. With a calendar it is easy to see why I have been left alone for two days—Saturday and Sunday. I spend the weekend thinking of all the things that I didn't ask for on my *want list*: books, magazines, paper and pens, paints, a toothbrush, home. I would be happy to have a coloring book and a box of crayons, anything to take my mind away from the voices in my head. The voices are always there, waiting for a quiet time to break through. Once the words start, I can't turn them off.

I hate you.

I hate you, too.

I've always hated you.

Pooooor Robbie.

And the last words, the ones that chill me: *I'm going to kill you.*

I want to run, but I am trapped. I measure my room:

Walking heel-to-toe, it is 14 steps wide and 30 steps long.

I climb onto my desk and leap to my bed, somersault off the edge of the bed. If only I could run. Run away from Mr. Lester and his lists. Run away from Great Oaks. Run home, or to Grandma's house.

What will my next list be? I'll never score 100 percent again. Does that mean less food after today? Will Mr. Lester make me go back to that group? Why did he make me talk to a bunch of older kids?

Run. Run. Run. I have to run. *It's what a runner does when he's not running that makes him a champion.* I push my desk to the wall, stand in the center of the room, and run in place.

I get into a steady rhythm, legs lifting high, arms swinging to the ceiling. I close my eyes and pretended I'm running for real. Really running, outside and free.

RIVER FALLS

Ryan reached for the photo album.

"Wait." I pulled it back. "Let me explain it to you first."

"So explain."

"When I was nine, I got a new bike for my birthday." I opened the album and let Ryan see the first few pictures of the bike. "A few days later, when I wanted to ride, my parents wouldn't let me. They were too busy to watch and didn't think it was safe for me to go alone. So I snuck out."

"You rode your bike without permission? That's the big lie?"

"No, that's nothing. I rode it all over the subdivision and coasted down the hill next to the pro shop. I smashed into a parked car at the end of the street. Crushed my tire under the bumper, right behind a rear wheel, and landed on the trunk."

Ryan stared at me wide-eyed, then flipped a few pages of the book.

"There's no pictures of that. My front wheel was smashed and wasn't even attached to my bike. I..." The rest wasn't easy to talk about.

"What did your dad say?"

"He doesn't know. I threw the bike into the Dumpster behind the pro shop. When Dad asked me where it was a few days later, I pretended to be surprised it wasn't in the garage." I took a deep breath. "My parents think it was stolen."

"You stole your own bike?"

"I guess."

I tucked the book back into its hiding place and turned out the light.

Sometime in the middle of the night, Ryan shook me. "I just heard your parents go to bed. Now we can get out of here."

"We can't go anywhere. Our house has a burglar alarm."

"We're not breaking in. We're leaving. Don't you have a key?"

Ryan was so dumb about some things. "The alarm will go off when we open the door. Even from the inside."

"Well, what about the windows?"

"Them, too."

"Why didn't you tell me?" He punched my bed.

"Robbie? Ryan? Are you boys still awake?" called Mom.

We both made fake snores really loud.

"It's after midnight. Get to sleep!" yelled Dad.

When I started to fall asleep, Ryan said, "Call your dad. Tell him we have to go outside and look at the stars."

"What?"

"Tell him we have to look at the stars for homework. We'll sneak away." Ryan stood up and pulled on his jeans. "Go on."

"It's summer. We don't have homework." Sneak away from Dad. How did he expect to do that? "Why do you even want to go into the construction site anyway? Why do we have to go at night?"

"I told you. They won't let me in during the day."

"But..."

"I hate this boring town. I have to get in. Ask your dad."

I shook my head.

"Robbie, please?"

"No."

"Can't you do anything?" He opened my bedroom door. "Mr. Thompson. Mr. Thompson."

Our house was quiet.

Ryan stepped out into the hallway. "Missssteeerrr Thooooo-oompsooooon!"

Dad stomped down the hall, his feet pounding in the dark. "What's going on here?"

Ryan wasn't scared of my huge Dad; he looked so small and Dad was like a giant. Ryan made his voice all proper. "I'm sorry if I woke you, but—"

"Of course you woke me!" Dad snapped.

"We just remembered there's something we have to do for school, outside. We have to look at the stars."

Dad slapped the light on. "Is this true, Robbie? You have to look at the stars in the middle of the night?"

Ryan answered. "We can't see them in the daytime."

Ryan obviously knew nothing about talking back. We were going to get into huge trouble. No, Ryan was the guest, he was probably safe. I was going to get into trouble for sure.

Dad slapped the wall above the light switch to get our attention. He pointed his finger at Ryan. "You. Be. Quiet." He turned to me. "It's summer. You really have to do this for school?"

I sat up in bed, took a deep breath, and lied to my dad. "We almost forgot. There are certain stars and planets that you can't see all the time."

"Well, this is not the time to inform me about this." He glared at Ryan. "Don't disturb my sleep." Dad stomped away, his feet booming on every step.

Ryan cried softly into his pillow. I didn't know if it was because of my Dad being mean or because he couldn't get into the construction site.

"Sorry," I whispered.

Ryan didn't answer.

"Ryan, it's your turn now. Tell me something no one else knows."

Ryan took a deep breath. "My mom's been in the hospital a really long time."

GREAT OAKS ~~SCHOOL~~ PRISON

Monday morning, Mr. Lester warned me about the three rules of Group:

1. Always tell the truth. "If we don't believe you, we'll call a 'triple T' and that's your last chance. Tell The Truth."
2. When someone asks you a question, answer it. Don't dodge the issue.
3. Respect everyone.

The guy is a maniac. He expects a bunch of teenage criminals to respect me, a murderer? And I'm supposed to respect a hacker guy and an armed robber?

Mr. Lester nods, like he's giving me time to let it all sink in. "These guys are the closest kids to your age, Robbie. Even more important, they're all on the right track to get out of here. We can't just keep you in your room all the time. You'll never get home that way."

We walk up the stairs and I wonder how talking to a group of thugs is supposed to get me home. "How old are they?"

"Fifteen. Oh, Curtis just had a birthday, he's sixteen."

Mr. Lester opens group by asking, "What did everyone do this weekend?"

I say, "Nothing." It's the truth. I sink back in my chair and try to be forgotten.

Mr. Lester nods and looks at 76. 76 lets out a long breath and says, "Sat around all weekend, staring at the TV and losing at Ping-Pong."

Nelson smiles. He says, "I have a potential job interview that meets your requirements."

Mr. Lester raises his eyebrows.

Big fidgets in his chair like a kid waiting his turn. "Saw my boy. His mama caught a ride with Grams. Saw him Saturday afternoon and Sunday morning. He's walking now. Walks like a boxer. He called me 'Da.' Junior is smart, not even one and he's walking and talking like a champ."

Mr. Lester holds up his hands, otherwise Big would never stop blabbing.

I add up a list in my head. Weekend activities:

1. Nelson—researched jobs. He probably used a computer or at least a newspaper. Maybe he can even make phone calls.
2. 76—watched TV and played Ping-Pong.
3. Big—had a visitor
4. Me—nothing

Mr. Lester zeroes in on 76. "Are you going to tell me why your hand is bandaged up?"

"Not if I don't have to," says 76. He looks around for someone else to talk, but the rest of us stay silent.

Mr. Lester leans forward. "Vincent, tell me what happened to your hand."

76 says, "I bumped it on the wall."

Mr. Lester takes a deep breath. "Explain."

76 groans like his hand is really hurting. "My girl. I gotta get home. She's missin' me so bad, she's running around with jerks

in my pack. I used all my tokens to call her and she didn't hardly answer her cell." He looks up at Mr. Lester. "It's all your fault, keeping me here. When you gonna let me out?"

Mr. Lester says, "Dropping the subject of your hand for a moment, everyone knows what it takes to get out of here. All you have to do is do it."

I clear my throat. Everyone looks at me. "I don't know what it takes for me to get out or to have visitors or use the phone."

There is a thud, like something big falling against the door, and some muffled thumps from across the room. The door flies open so forcefully it bangs the wall. A kid as big as a house stands glaring at us. His legs almost touch either side of the doorway.

"Why didn't any of you fools come get me for group?"

Mr. Lester stands up. The body-builder boy doesn't seem to notice.

"Now I'm gonna lose tokens." He narrows his eyes. His face flushes pink.

"Who's that?" I whisper to 76.

He slouches down. Barely moving his lips, he whispers, "He's The Beef."

Mr. Lester says, "The Beef, this isn't your group. You left, remember?"

"I'm ready to come back."

Mr. Lester points to the door. "Glad to hear it, but your place has been taken. I'll keep you in mind for a new group. Leave now so we can get to work."

The Beef doesn't move a muscle. His eyes zoom in on me. In three steps he's in front of my chair. "Who are you? You're in my place! Get out!"

I scoot my chair back. Mr. Lester shoves his way between us. "The Beef, leave now."

"If I leave, he's comin' with me." The Beef points at me.

Mr. Lester bends his neck way down and talks into his collar.

"Five-one, fifth floor, room twelve. Five-one, plus three. Fifth floor, room twelve."

The Beef steps back. "What did you do that for? You called a five-one on me?"

Big, 76, and Nelson waltz to the far end of the room. I jump up and follow. "What's a five-one?" I whisper.

"Shut up, kid," says 76, eyeing the door.

RIVER FALLS

Dad found a way to make us pay for waking him last night. He ordered us to clean out the garage.

I grabbed the garage remote from the shelf where Dad kept his keys, and we headed outside. Ryan held out his hand like a little kid. "Can I push it?" I handed him the remote and we watched the door click up. "I don't have to help, you know."

"Yes, you do. My dad said."

"He's not my dad. He can't make me do anything."

I opened the storage boxes with my stuff and started throwing things away.

Ryan just watched.

I threw out two broken skateboards, notebooks, dried paint, and even a few old broken toys.

Dad actually looked impressed when I told him we'd finished. "You boys already cleaned out the whole garage?"

"Not the *whole* garage, just my stuff."

He led us back and pointed out everything he wanted us to haul away—the glass bottles, old plastic jugs, wooden crates filled with scraps of wood, broken ceramic pots. I wanted to complain, to tell him that it wasn't our—my—stuff. But complaining wouldn't help.

And we actually did uncover a few really cool things—one of Uncle Grant's old punching bags and a camping tent that was practically new.

Ryan and I loaded the junk onto my old wagon and made trips to the subdivision's recycling center behind the pro shop. We took turns pulling the wagon. As Ryan was pulling it uphill, he looked back a few times. "You sure don't know how to take care of anything. Two skateboards, two *broken* skateboards."

The recycling area smelled like rotten fruit; there was broken glass and even a few bottles that didn't make it into the glass recycling. Ryan tossed the glass hard into the bottom of the container, trying to break every bottle and jar that he threw.

When Ryan finished shattering glass, we heard a low whining noise, like a squeaky screen door. We found the noise behind the wood recycling bin. Two tiny kittens were curled up in the long grass. I started to reach for them and Ryan pulled me away.

"They're too little to touch. Get back."

"They won't hurt me." I took a step closer.

Ryan blocked my path. "You will hurt them. Their mom is probably moving the whole litter, she won't want them with your smell on their fur. Get back."

I kept my eye on the kittens and walked with Ryan until we were hidden behind the bin with scrap metal. A few minutes later, a cat came and picked up one of the kittens. When she left, the last lone kitten began to meow as loud as a full-grown cat.

"How did you know?" I asked Ryan.

Just then we heard laughing, and some older kids rounded the corner and circled the kitten. "Big mouth for a little cat," said the tallest boy. It was Buckley West. He was taller and his hair was longer than when he went to Red Brick Elementary. The other two boys with him didn't say anything.

Ryan started to stand and defend the kitten. "No," I leaned in and whispered. "That's Buckley West. He's . . . scary."

Buckley bent over and picked up the newborn kitten. Ryan stood up. "Don't touch him. Put him down."

Buckley laughed and held the kitten high. "This your cat?"

"Just put him down; his mom's coming for him."

"Here, catch." Buckley tossed the kitten to one of his friends.

The kitten's meow turned into a wail. The three of them tossed the kitten back and forth, ignoring Ryan.

Ryan reached into the metal recycling bin. "I said put it down."

Ryan tossed a flattened can at Buckley. It whirled through the air like a Frisbee and hit him square on the forehead. Buckley froze. Ryan didn't stop; as soon as his right hand released a piece of metal he dug his left hand into the bin for his next weapon. He let loose on all three boys. I was scared, but I stood up. I concentrated on finding Ryan the best metal pieces. We had to save the kitten.

As soon as Buckley and his friends recovered from their shock that a kid like Ryan actually started a fight with all three of them, they went on the attack. "He hit me," Buckley growled. "The kid hit me." Buckley dropped the kitten. It disappeared in the long grass. The older kids grabbed the cans and scraps that had fallen around them and hurled some back at us. "Let's get him!" Buckley roared.

"Ryan! Run!"

We left my wagon behind and sprinted to my house. Buckley and his followers ran behind us for two blocks. They tried to throw some more junk at us, but they missed.

Later, I wanted to go check on the kitten.

"He won't be there," Ryan said.

"How do you know?"

"I just know. We won't find him. Either his mom took him, or she didn't. If she took him, he has a chance."

"At least you tried," I told Ryan. At least someone stood up to Buckley West. Dylan and Tyler would have never done something like that.

After Ryan left, I went to get my wagon from the recycling center. I found the spot where Buckley and his friends had stood, still littered with metal scraps. There was no sign of the kitten. I searched the field and even looked into the recycling containers. Maybe the mother cat did come back for him.

Maybe he did have a chance.

GREAT OAKS ~~SCHOOL~~ PRISON

The Beef shakes his head at Mr. Lester. "You think five of you can take me? Think again."

A stream of men in green coveralls pour through the door. The guy in the lead is a mountain of muscle. "Team of four," he says to Mr. Lester. "What's the plan?"

"We wait for the plus three," says Mr. Lester. Just then three more guys run in. One of them is Big Nose.

"We don't have to do this," says The Beef. "Everything's under control here." But no one is listening to him, they are whispering together.

They fan out and surround The Beef.

Mr. Lester says, "Okay. Team one. On seven. My count."

The Beef says, "No."

Mr. Lester counts. "One...two—"

Mr. Lester and four other guys rush at The Beef. They pin him down on the floor before the rest of us realize he didn't count to seven, didn't even say three. Two coverall guys hold down The Beef's feet, two more hold his hands, and Mr. Lester is leaning on The Beef's ear, keeping his head close to the floor. Three more men circle around.

Big Nose pushes a button on his stopwatch. "I got the time," he says. "You know the drill, The Beef. Two minutes."

The Beef doesn't move at all, not even a wiggle. After two minutes, Mr. Lester nods to the other four guys. They tighten their hold on The Beef's hands and feet. Mr. Lester lets go of The Beef's head. "Head is free," says Mr. Lester.

He tells The Beef, "Nicely done."

The Beef lifts his head and looks past Mr. Lester, at me. "I'm gonna kill you, kid."

Mr. Lester shoves The Beef's head back down. Big Nose's stopwatch beeps as he changes the settings. "Phase two, five minutes," he says.

I can't tear my eyes away from The Beef. For the past few weeks, I felt that being locked in my small room was the worst punishment. Now right in front of my eyes is something I've never imagined. A part of me wants to scream at the men to let the kid up. But since The Beef wants to kill me, I'm glad it is impossible for him to get me.

The men holding The Beef are still as statues. I shift my weight from my right foot to my left foot and back again, like a little kid who has to pee. I hear Big and 76 taking deep breaths next to me and the soft whistle as 76 exhales out of his nose. I try but I can't manage a deep breath. It's hard enough to stay against the wall. I don't want to watch, but my eyes dart from one pair of hands to another, each gripping one of The Beef's wrists or ankles. And Mr. Lester's hands pressed against The Beef's cheek and ear, anchoring his head to the floor.

After five minutes, The Beef's head is released again. His face is flushed and he's breathing heavy as though lying still is a lot of work. He glares at me and chokes out, "I'll kill you dead!"

Mr. Lester says, "Clear the room."

Me, Big, 76, and Nelson can't get out fast enough. They head left to go to their rooms. I open the door to the stairwell as Big Nose says, "Ten minutes."

I walk downstairs alone to my empty room and close the door behind me.

RIVER FALLS

Whenever Ryan didn't show up in time for breakfast, I couldn't help but wonder if he'd been at the construction site the night before, wonder if he was at home sleeping, or if he had been caught by the construction guys, or the police.

Twice I walked to the corner of Howell and Pine and found Ryan walking down the street on his way to our house. I'd let out a sigh of relief that I didn't have to walk up to 111 Howell Street and knock on the door.

I gave Mom and Dad a few days to forget about the trouble Ryan caused, and asked if he could spend the night again. Dylan wasn't answering my e-mails; he was still at space camp. It felt like he was actually in outer space. When I called Tyler's house, his dad told me he was with his mom for the rest of the summer.

Dad looked at me over the top of his glasses and shook his head. "Ryan sleep here again? You can't be serious. That was a disaster."

"We wouldn't bother you at all. The tent, remember? You said we could set it up in the backyard."

Dad helped us set it up without promising that Ryan could stay over. Ryan and I swept out the tent and put some old sleeping bags in it. Just before dinner Ryan cleared his throat.

"I'm really sorry." He looked first at Dad and then at Mom. "For wanting to look at the stars and for waking you up."

After dinner, when Dad usually walked Ryan home, he said,

"Let's call your grandparents, see if they can spare you one more night."

Around midnight, all the lights went out in the house.

"Let's go, Robbie. No alarms tonight."

"I don't know." I'd thought about it, sneaking out, walking around town with Ryan.

"It might be our last chance ever."

I wasn't obsessed with the construction site, like Ryan, but part of me wanted to go just to see what it would be like. I didn't want to get into trouble. "What if someone sees us?"

"There's nothing to worry about. I've done this before. Just follow my lead."

He made it sound simple, like telling me how to jump from the high dive and free fall from my desk to my mattress. I followed him out of the tent.

At the construction site, Ryan tried to squeeze between the gate and the fence. He tried to pry the lock open with a paper clip.

"That only works on TV," I told him.

"Well, what's your idea?" Ryan threw the paper clip down and started climbing the fence. He slowed as he reached the big roll of sharp wire at the top, the stuff you see on prison fences in the movies.

"Owww!" Ryan screamed. He hopped down, swinging away from the fence, holding one hand out. When he reached the ground he waved a bloody hand in my face and said, "Take off your shirt."

"The mosquitoes, they'll eat me alive."

"I'm bleeding!" He reached for my shirt with his bloody hand.

I peeled it off. He grabbed it and climbed up the fence again. When he got to the top he flung my shirt on the sharp wire and tried to swing his leg over top of it.

"Owww! Yeee-owww!" Ryan slid down the fence and landed on his back. "Owww. My leg. My back. My hand. My leg."

I stood over him wondering if I should go for help or try to lift him somehow. He rolled to his side and managed to stand. Ryan hopped on one foot and rubbed the inside of his other leg with his good hand. "That fence nearly took my leg off. That razor wire is as sharp as glass. That fence—"

"Still has my shirt," I said.

Ryan was still hopping. "I can't climb up there."

I climbed up the giant fence. The tiny razor-sharp spikes in the wire bit into the cloth. When I tugged, my shirt ripped to shreds. I took half a shirt home with me and used it to swat mosquitoes. The other half waved from the top of the fence like a surrender flag.

GREAT OAKS ~~SCHOOL~~ PRISON

I walk to group with Mr. Lester the next day, knowing there is a giant boy on the fifth floor who wants to kill me.

In group, Mr. Lester says, "Robbie, tell everyone how you came to be at Great Oaks."

"It didn't work out at the other schools," I say.

Nelson snorts. 76 stifles a laugh. "Guess not. You being a mass murderer and all."

"I'm not a mass murderer," I grumble. "I killed one little punk, a dirty rotten thief!" They are all quiet. "But I guess you think it's okay to be a thief since you've done it 78 times. Pointed a gun at people, made them give you their stuff."

"No. You got it wrong, I didn't—"

Mr. Lester cuts him off. "Robbie, we are to be respectful of everyone in the group."

"Respectful? He called me a mass murderer."

"Okay. Triple T," says Mr. Lester. "Vincent, you first."

"Yo, Robbie man. I didn't threaten no one with no gun. It wasn't like that."

"A knife then." I am not stupid. I know "armed robbery" means you use a weapon.

"No." 76 slouches in his chair. "It was on account of our dogs. Our pack, we walk the streets with our dogs, for our own protection. When things went down, it all got pinned on the dogs being dangerous. So the courts made it out to be armed robbery. I mean it wasn't nothing but a little street fight, that's all."

He is lying. I can tell. No kid could wind up in here just for getting into a fight.

But Mr. Lester seems satisfied with the lie. "Robbie? Your turn, triple T."

"This kid stole stuff from us." My chest tightens. "I couldn't stand him, hated him." My heart speeds up, slows down; it tries to climb up my chest and out of my throat. I shrug to show I don't care at all. "I beat the crap out of him. He died. That's all."

"You shut him down, just for taking stuff?" Nelson shakes his head. "That's so not right. Stuff is just stuff. A life is a life."

I remember he's a computer hacker, a geek who breaks into computer systems, drains people's bank accounts. He is scum, just like 76. "Well, I guess you thieves all stick together. How much money did you steal from all those computers you hacked?"

"Robbie. Respectful. This is your second warning." Mr. Lester sounds like a kindergarten teacher.

"Money? I didn't steal any money. I broke into computers for my own education."

Every single person in this room is a liar.

Including me.

RIVER FALLS

Mom worried about us sleeping in the tent. "You're covered with mosquito bites." She held a timer in her hands waiting for it to go off.

"Same as any summer." I glanced through the oven window. Blueberry muffins.

"Sleeping on the ground can't be good for your health. And Ryan's had a terrible limp for two days."

"I'm fine. We're both fine."

"Really, I think it can permanently damage your back." She looked me up and down as if her eyes were strong enough to see a broken spine through my skin.

"Mom, I would notice if my back hurt."

"I'm happy that you're spending time with Ryan, but you're ignoring your other friends."

"Dylan and Tyler are out of town."

"Well, those two aren't your only friends," she said. From the side door I heard a girl giggle. "Come on in, Anna Beth."

"What is she doing here?"

Mom ran a knife around the edges of the muffins. "She's here for breakfast and she's volunteered to read with the toddlers today."

"Have fun," I said. I grabbed a muffin and sat on the swing to wait for Ryan.

Anna Beth left and I was still waiting for Ryan. I walked to the corner of Pine and Howell, no Ryan. I walked down Howell Street and stood in front of 111, no Ryan.

His grandfather sat on the porch with his elbows on his knees.

"Is Ryan here?" I called from the sidewalk.

"Boy." He coughed and spat on the porch. "Boy? Get on out here. Your friend's here."

Ryan flew out the door and squeezed past his grandfather and down the steps.

"Where have you been all morning?"

"Here. Why?" Ryan bent down to tie his shoe. His shoelaces were different colors.

"It's way past breakfast. I just wanted to make sure you were coming over, that's all."

Ryan stood up. "Of course I am."

That night, it was so hot that we left the flaps of the tent open. Ryan pulled a giant pair of garden shears out from under his pillow. "We're getting in tonight, for sure."

"Go ahead if you want," I told him. "I'm staying here."

Ryan was silent awhile.

I shone my flashlight on him. "My mom's acting all weird, like she might check on us."

"Robbie, you *need* to come with me. You need excitement in your life."

"Finishing a race, running across the finish line, that's my idea of exciting. Watching you almost cut your leg off on the fence is not."

"Stay here and be a safe little baby, Robbie. I'm going to have fun." Without waiting for Mom and Dad to turn out the lights, he slipped out of the tent and ran across the yard.

I lay back on my sleeping bag. If Uncle Grant were here, he'd get Dad to leave the fire in the BBQ going. He'd tell us ghost stories. Ryan wouldn't have to sneak out to have fun.

I went inside for water. Mom was watching TV. Dad was hunched over some papers.

"I just came in to say good night," I said.

"You and Ryan okay?" asked Mom. But it wasn't really a question; she didn't take her eyes from the TV screen.

Dad looked over at me and smiled. "I'm glad Ryan got me to pull that tent out of the garage. He has a real sense of adventure, that boy." *If he only knew.*

"Night," I said, taking a bottle of water.

Ryan wasn't gone long. He slid into the tent and stretched out on his sleeping bag. Two things told me that he didn't get in: the clippers were nowhere to be seen and Ryan was too quiet. So quiet I could barely hear him breathe.

When I was drifting off to sleep, Ryan said, "You should have come with me."

"Why?"

"Because that's what friends do. They help each other."

GREAT OAKS ~~SCHOOL~~ PRISON

When Mr. Lester leads me to my room, I ask, "Why do you lock me down here in my room alone while the other guys get everything?"

"They do not get *everything*, Robbie."

"Yes, they do. They get phone calls, visitors, Ping-Pong, everything."

"You named three things. Three things are not everything." Mr. Lester leans against my wall. "Ask me a logical question or we are done speaking for now."

"Why can't I live upstairs?" I hope it's logical.

"Two reasons. One, I'm not sure if you're ready. And two, someone up there has threatened you."

The Beef.

"But that's not my fault! Just because he threatens me, I have to be locked up? That's totally not fair."

Mr. Lester holds up his hands, like he did when Big went on and on about his baby. "Robbie, stop. There were two parts to that problem. Focus on what you can do. Let us handle The Beef."

"What can I do?"

Mr. Lester smiles like I've just given him a box of money. "Now we're talking," he says. "Wait here." He walks away, leaving my door wide open.

Mr. Lester comes back with a bunch of big brown envelopes bundled together by a huge rubber band. "I was trying to keep these in order. They're all mixed up now." He sets them on the end of my bed. "Letters from home. Read."

RIVER FALLS

To: Robbie Thompson
From: Grant Reynolds
I'm still loving the heat. Went to a market bazaar the other day. It was amazing. Time for me to grab some grub. It's all good.
See you later, Uncle Grant

I had just finished sending e-mails to Uncle Grant, to Tyler in California, and to Dylan at space camp. I opened up my photo folder of nose close-ups, pus mountain pictures, and other weird close-up shots from Uncle Grant's party. I made a wicked discovery with the red-eye feature on FotoFixer: dots appear anywhere on the photos, not just the eyes. I created a blue zit pus mountain and a gray zit pus mountain, and was trying to figure out how to make rainbow pox.

Dad snuck up behind me. "What are you doing?"

I closed my picture without saving it. "Nothing."

Dad cleared his throat. "So are you all ready for the race tomorrow? It's another long one."

"I'm ready. Will you come?"

"Robbie." His voice was impatient like when we used to shot hoops and he acted like I wasn't even trying to get the ball in. "We've been over this before."

Mom called, "Robbie, Ryan's coming up."

Dad said, "I'll try, okay? That's all anyone can do is try, right?"

Maybe. But when it came to watching me cross the finish line, Dad didn't seem to try hard enough.

Ryan stepped into the room just as Dad left.

"What was that all about?" Ryan asked. "Who's trying to do what?"

"Dad said he'd try to come to my race tomorrow." I closed the photo program. "But he won't. He never does."

Ryan dug into a plastic bag, brought out two small shovels, and set them on my desk. "We'll dig our way in," he said with the hugest smile ever.

I flopped down on my bed. "No way. I told you I don't want to do it."

Ryan tapped the shovels together like he was making music. "It would take me forever to dig it on my own. Help me. Say you'll help me."

"My race is tomorrow. I couldn't do it tonight even if I did want to."

Ryan stopped tapping and put the shovels back in the bag. "I can wait one more night."

GREAT OAKS ~~SCHOOL~~ PRISON

Inside each of the big envelopes I find letters and cards from Mom, Dad, Grandma and Uncle Grant. Every letter has already been opened. Mr. Lester has read all my letters, I am sure of it. Probably anyone who works at Great Oaks had a chance to read them. I pour out all the letters and push them into a big pile. I want to read them. And I don't want to read them.

I pull out the big padded envelopes first. They are all from Mom. Short notes saying she sent me things: magazines, comic books, and candy. But there is nothing, just Mom's letters.

Mr. Lester will be getting a list. A list of stuff Mom sent and people at Great Oaks stole. I arrange the letters by the date they were sent and start reading at the beginning. They all say the same thing a bunch of different ways. *Miss you. Hope you are doing well. When are you coming home?*

I could answer a whole hundred letters in a few words: "Me too," "I'm okay," and "I don't know."

The letters don't say "Are you still crazy?" or "Have you finally finished making a mess of your life?"

Dad sent a bunch of cards. Joke cards, get-well-soon cards, and miss-you cards. I guess the store didn't have a juvenile-delinquent card section. Someone should invent cards like that for locked-up kids—adults, too. *Sorry you're in jail. Hope you get out soon.*

Grant sent cards, too. They had drawings on the front and

he wrote inside them. In almost every card he says he sent photos. There are no pictures in the cards. Mr. Lester is going to hear about this.

Grandma sent riddles from fortune cookies. Some are funny, others are strange. One says, *What does a smart person do in an impossible situation?*

I try to figure that one out. Give up? Get away? I turn the paper over and read: *The impossible.* If Grandma had said something like that before, I probably would have just looked at her like she was crazy and said, "Whatever, Grandma." But after living at Great Oaks, the riddle makes perfect sense.

Mom wrote long letters, almost too long. She wrote about the weather and the flowers that were blooming. That's the boring stuff I skip when I read books. She also wrote about the daycare, what every single kid was dong. One kid fell out of bed and hurt her head just like the monkeys jumping on the bed. *She's fine now, thank goodness,* Mom wrote. She ended all her letters with the words: *You are missed. Love, Mom.*

Even though her letters are long and a little boring, Mom's letters make me remember home most. Her writing is the same handwriting I used to see each morning scribbled on the Mega Calendar on the fridge. Reading about the daycare, I can hear the kids fighting, babies crying, and toys screaming out music.

I'm crying by the time I reach for the last envelope, which Mom sent two days ago. I miss home so much, it is so totally unfair.

I pull out one piece of paper, short for one of Mom's letters.

Dear Robbie,

We all miss you, Son. I've been calling for two weeks.

Trying to plan a visit, but they won't let us schedule one. Not even for a family meeting. We're told it could interfere with your progress.

I'm glad to know that you are making progress, but I wish I could hear it from you.

Please write to us when you get a chance. I am worried that I haven't heard from you. I've told your father that the only reason I can think of that you wouldn't write or give us a quick call is that you are still living on the first floor for new kids and have no privileges. Dad tells me not to worry and that you are probably spending all your time at the gym and the rec room and maybe even signed up for the Great Oaks track team.

I wanted to make the drive over there to tell you this news in person, but now I'm running out of time. So here goes. It seems that you really are going to have a brother or sister in a few months. Everything is going well. I just have to take it easy until the baby gets here.

I can't wait until you're home and Dad and I can share the excitement with you. You are missed.

Love, Mom

A baby! Mom and Dad sure know what to do with their impossible situation! If your first child doesn't work out, replace him.

I grab a piece of paper and write:

Dear Mom and Dad,

Have another baby. I hope it's a boy. You can name him Robbie and forget all about me!

Robbie (the first one)

I try to sleep, try to tell myself that this new baby has nothing to do with me. Mom and Dad have wanted this for years. They aren't having a baby now because I am locked up in here. They aren't trying to forget all about me. I try to remember the feeling I had from all the other letters, before I'd read the last one. They miss me. They want me home.

But I can't make myself feel that way again. One word keeps popping into my head: *baby*.

RIVER FALLS

This 10K race was different from the last. Some of the runners had uniforms. They ran with a team or club. I found a good place to stretch and read the shirts of the people who walked by:

> *End Childhood Cancer*
> *TriCounty Suicide Prevention*
> *Breast Cancer Awareness*
> *Ask Me About Autism*

The whole event seemed bigger, brighter, better, somehow more important than any other race I'd ever run.

I didn't start too fast this time. At the eight-kilometer mark, I started to hit the wall. Hitting the wall is the running term for feeling like you can't go any farther. A guy ahead of me ran with a string around his wrist. A few feet away, a lady in a red shirt ran next to him. The other end of the string was tied to her wrist. The back of the guy's shirt read: *You don't need sight to have vision.* I read it over and over, pounding out the words with my footfalls. *You don't need sight to have vision.* It hit me—the runner was blind. He didn't have *sight* but he had *vision*, a vision to finish the race.

I ran behind them for a while trying to figure out how the string between their wrists guided the blind runner. The lady must talk to him, too. Or how would he know if there was a hill or a step or something that he might trip over?

The road ahead was clear and level. *What did it feel like to be blind?* I closed my eyes for a few strides and felt my stomach sink like I was on a carnival ride. My ankle wobbled. My eyes flew open quick. How could I have been so stupid? I could have sprained my ankle, or maybe even broken a leg. Just thinking about my ankle made it hurt a little. I thought of the runners who got sidelined during a race. Most just stopped to clench their sides or walk with their hands over their heads because they were out of breath. But some ended up limping on blown-out knees.

Running could be dangerous. *Think of something else.*

Would Dad be at the finish line?

I slowed at a water stand and grabbed a paper cup. The man next to me poured his water over his head. It was hot, but I knew Uncle Grant was hotter out in the desert.

I heard people clapping and shouting and realized I was going to make it. The finish line had to be near with so many people cheering.

My legs were heavy, but the finish line was in sight. I'd have to look strong in case Dad was watching. People were watching me and that made me want to run my best. I focused on the finish line: the tables with water and juice and oranges and bagels past the finish line, a place to stretch and walk and eat and drink. I ran full speed ahead.

"Robbie! Robbie! Robbie! Robbie!" I didn't see Dad or Mom. But there were voices, kids' voice, and they were cheering for me.

I crossed the finish line running strong, slowed down to a trot, and walked. The crowd around the finish line was thick. I was too tired to smile and my muscles felt all jittery. Walking felt slow-motion and a lot of work. But my stomach was floaty and happy. A lady with pink lipstick gave me my medal.

I lifted my hands over my head to help me catch my breath and wandered around the finish. Suddenly I felt super hungry.

I grabbed a slice of orange and stuck it in my mouth with the peel still on.

Next to the orange table was a table with a sign that read: River Falls Ten Miler.

I thought of Uncle Grant. "If you can run 6.1 miles—twice—then you can run ten miles."

But could I?

There was only one way to find out. I signed my name on the registration form.

"Hey, Robbie! Over here!" I turned to the sound of Ryan's voice, but it wasn't just Ryan. There were about ten kids from school—Alex, Sam, Michael, Noah H and Noah S, my basketball buddies—and, jumping up and down in the back of the group, Anna Beth Carter.

"Robbie, you were totally the youngest kid running that race," said Michael.

"Wow, look at his medal," said Noah S.

"He's got lots of medals," said Ryan.

Mom and Grandma strolled up behind my friends. "Is Dad here?"

Mom shook her head. "He couldn't make it."

But so many kids from school came. Mom must have told them.

"What are you all doing here? How did you even know?"

"Anna Beth called me," said Alex.

"Me, too," said Sam.

Anna Beth wrinkled her nose. "Don't look at me; it was all Ryan's idea."

Ryan looked down at the ground, but his smile gave him away.

GREAT OAKS ~~SCHOOL~~ PRISON

Mr. Lester hands us each a cupcake. I sniff it and my mouth starts to water. I haven't had anything sweet since I got locked in here. He makes each of us stand up and review our progress. Everyone has something to celebrate except me. Big has a plan to get out of Great Oaks School (and it was approved by Mr. Lester), 76 is going to start classes, and Nelson has scored the jackpot. He's leaving Great Oaks and moving to Cedar House, a halfway house where he will go to school and work.

The cupcakes are in honor of Nelson. Mr. Lester has him pose with a certificate and takes a photograph.

This is nothing like a real group meeting at all, until Mr. Lester says, "What about you, Robbie? What have you done?"

A thousand comments come to my mind: *I do whatever you tell me to. Nothing, I'm locked in my room. I don't have a plan so I don't know what to do. Sit in my room, go crazy and rot away into nothing.*

I lick the icing on my cupcake. I don't answer him right away because my brain is fighting with itself. Part of it screams, *Tell him the truth! There is nothing* to *do.* But mostly my brain begs me to *think of something quick.*

"I don't know." I look around.

"That is not an acceptable answer."

That figures! "It's been hard. To stay here. I don't know if any of you know what it's like on the first floor."

Big's eyes widen. 76 and Nelson lean forward.

Mr. Lester lets out a huff. "They've all been on the first floor, Robbie. That's where everyone starts. What have *you* accomplished?"

76 stands up. "You're keeping him *there*? Day after day? In the torture chamber?"

Big says, "How long have you been there, kid?"

"Twenty-six and a half days."

Nelson and 76 say, "Firecracker." Big, too, but he says "Holy" first.

I peel the paper from my cupcake and take a bite.

76 crosses his arms. "That ain't right. Don't matter what he done; that ain't right."

Mr. Lester waves his arms trying to settle everyone down. "This is not a debate about school procedures. It is a discussion of our accomplishments." He points at me. "Robbie, you've written some fine lists. And in group, you admitted your offense." He glares at Big. "Admitting what you have done and taking responsibility for your actions is an important part of rehabilitation."

I nod. *Whatever.*

"However, I need to hold you to the truth. We let this story spin out of control. You say you're a murderer. The story grows into you becoming a mass murderer. We both know neither one is true, right, Robbie?"

"I never said I was a mass murderer! 76 said it."

"Reminder. Call Vincent by his proper name." Mr. Lester opens a folder and pulls out a piece of paper. "Your exact words were, 'I couldn't stand him, hated him. I beat the crap out of him. He died. That's all.' "

How did he know my exact words? Were they recording—or videotaping—in this room?

I shrug. "That's right."

Mr. Lester lifts another piece of paper and reads. "I didn't mean to do it. It was the worst accident in the world. We were fighting, but it was over. I was going to help him. He just fell. All on his own, he fell. I didn't even touch him, I swear."

When he finishes reading, everyone's eyes move from him to me.

"You know what that was, right, Robbie?"

I nod. "Yes."

Mr. Lester sits down. "Then please explain how the official police report from the day of Ryan's death is so very different from the story you told us in here."

"I told the police I didn't do it. What do you think, I'm stupid?"

Mr. Lester shakes his head. "I've never thought that, Robbie. I think at the time you were a twelve-year-old boy who was really afraid. Now you're a thirteen-year-old boy who is extremely angry. But stories do no good. Telling the truth and taking responsibility is what this is about. Come on, Robbie. Triple T."

"I told you the truth. I hated that kid and I killed him. End of story."

"The kid's name was Ryan, Robbie. Ryan."

I know his name. I look at the last half of my cupcake and don't want to take another bite.

"I'm not saying another firecracker thing."

Mr. Lester switches from his questioning voice to a teacher voice. "In that case we're done for today. Just one announcement. Now that we have an extra space in our group, I've invited The Beef to rejoin us."

RIVER FALLS

That night in the tent I expected Ryan to beg me to go to the construction site, but he was quiet.

"How did you get Anna Beth Carter to help you today?"

"I just told her she was smart and that everyone always listens to her. She's easy to persuade."

"When I saw everyone from class, I couldn't believe it."

Ryan coughed. "I tried to get your dad to come."

"What? How?"

"I just called and asked him. And I called back to remind him."

"You called my dad? At work?"

Ryan nodded. "Five times." He tapped his two shovels together. "I'm not sure if I'll get in this time, but I have to try."

I warned him it was breaking and entering or stealing.

"I'm not taking anything. I'm not breaking anything. I'm just moving dirt from one place to another. Moving dirt isn't against the law."

I gave him a bunch of reasons not to go. He could get caught, or hurt, or stuck even.

"So help me then. Be my lookout. Or dig, just a little bit."

The shovels were so little; digging took forever. We found a smooth flat area at the back of the lot, but the dirt was hard as stone. We swung the tips of the shovels straight down to loosen the dirt, but each shovelful only cleared away the top crumbs.

After a while we got down to softer dirt and Ryan dug fast, leaning under the fence and scooping dirt with the shovel. The spokes at the bottom of the fence dug long scratches into Ryan's arms.

"You're bleeding," I told him.

"I don't care."

"You don't *care* that you're *bleeding*?"

Ryan dug faster. "That's right." He lay down to test the hole and glanced at me. "Your legs hurt but you ran the race anyway, right?"

I kept digging.

He was able to fit his arm and shoulder through the hole. "Almost finished." Ryan dug faster than ever.

"I'm helping you dig, but I'm not going in." I pushed on the tiny shovel so hard the handle bent.

Ryan stood and bent over the hole. He tossed his shovel to the side and scooped dirt out with his hands like a dog digging under a fence. The dirt flew under his legs. "It's gonna work!"

It wasn't long before Ryan stopped digging and smiled. "It's ready."

GREAT OAKS ~~SCHOOL~~ PRISON

The Beef slouches in an oversize chair, Big and 76 sit across from him. I keep my eyes on my plastic slippers and walk to my seat without even glancing in his direction, glad that Mr. Lester sits between us. Mr. Lester grills me right from the start. "Robbie, have you thought about our discussion from last time?"

My only thought has been to wonder how many minutes I would stay alive in the same room as The Beef. "Yes, sir," I say. "I was thinking that I'd like to know Big's plan to get out of here, or how to make one of my own."

The Beef laughs. "Wouldn't we all, ya firecracker for brains."

I ignore him and look at Mr. Lester. "Robbie, I'll remind you to use proper names for people in this group. The Beef, be respectful of others, this is your first warning."

"Proper names? Why can't I call Big, Big and 76, 76? You're calling him The Beef."

The Beef shoots out of his chair and leans over me. "You making fun of my name?" His pale face is splotched with pink.

Mr. Lester stands between us. "The Beef, your goal is to control your anger; please sit down." He places one hand in the center of The Beef's chest and guides him to his chair. Mr. Lester sits down and says to me, "The Beef is our newest group member's proper name."

No way! I'm overcome with a floaty, giggly feeling. I bite my bottom lip to stop myself from laughing. *What does it matter? If*

Mr. Lester won't help me get out of here, at least I can screw up The Beef's day. His goal is to control his anger.

"Your parents named you 'The'?" I ask.

"Shut up, kid," warns 76.

The Beef stands up. Now that I've started, I can't slow down. "I mean, why not 'Rare'?" Everyone's eyes are on me, begging me to stop, but I can't. "Or 'Roast' or 'Chopped' or 'Ground'?"

I'm falling. My chair is falling, tilting back. I fly backward and fall in slow motion.

76 says, "No!"

Mr. Lester yells, "Stop!"

A moment before my head hits the floor, I realize The Beef has snuck behind me and launched an attack.

RIVER FALLS

I lay on my back, feeling the wetness of the newly dug dirt through my shirt and smelling the worm smell like the air after a rain. *I should be in the tent right now. I should be asleep. I should be anyplace but here.* Half of my body was already in the construction site, but the rest of me was trying to pull myself back to reality, back home.

"Roooobbbbbiiiiiieeeeeeeeeeeeee," Ryan called. "Robbie! Robbie! Robbie!"

I slid under the fence and stood up. I couldn't see Ryan, but I could hear him. "Rob-bie! Rob-bie!"

"Shut up! Someone will hear you!" I half yelled, half hissed at him and made my way around ruts to the sound of Ryan's voice.

"Robbie is a scaredy cat. Meow! Meow!" He'd managed to climb up on the seat of the bulldozer. If he could climb it, I could climb it.

"Check this out. This is me. I'm going to work construction, right after I finish fighting in the war."

I got into the seat with him. Every time a car drove by, I ducked.

Ryan laughed. "No one's gonna catch us. All the nights I've come up here, I never saw anyone and no one saw me."

"You probably weren't so loud before, either."

Ryan stood up. He pretended to pull the controls. "Crrrsssuuuussshhhhhhhh! Bam! I'll destroy everything. I could run this thing into buildings and knock them down." He was pretending, like a preschool kid with dump trucks and Legos.

A little red car drove by extra slow. "Ryan, let's go."

"We just got here."

The car circled around and stopped. "Ryan, someone's here." I ducked again.

Ryan laughed. "How would you know from down there? There's no one here, really." He started to rev up his voice for another round of construction make-believe, but his sound effects were drowned out by sirens.

Three police cars zoomed to the main entrance of the site. Ryan flew down and bolted away.

"Hey! Stop!" The police officer's voice was loud and clear.

I slid to the fence and rolled onto my back. Police officers were rounding the fence from each direction. The bottom of the fence slashed across my chest as I escaped. When I stood up, I glanced around for Ryan. He had disappeared.

One of the policemen caught me in the flashlight beam. I took off running and heard a policewoman's voice. "He's over there. White T-shirt. Blue jeans. Small." For a moment, I almost stopped and put my hands up. Instead, I ran up the hill to the strip mall and sprinted behind it. I ran down the side streets off Main and cut between houses. I ran until I couldn't hear the police officers or their sirens. I flew down my street and it felt like I was the only living thing, the only moving thing, in a pretend world. Every leaf on every tree seemed frozen; time stopped just long enough for me to get home.

I dived into the tent arms-first, sliding on my stomach like a baseball player crossing home plate. The scrapes on my chest burned. My heart thumped like crazy.

It was a long while before my heart and breath relaxed and fit back in my chest again. My ears still tried to detect sirens. Little by little the tiny muscles in my calves, my shoulders, and my back cramped up. I lay awake almost the entire night, listening for the sirens and wondering if the police would be coming for me.

Ryan was sitting outside the tent before sunrise. He was clean but wearing the same clothes he had on last night, dirty jeans and a gray T-shirt smeared with reddish-brown dirt from the construction site. He smelled like lemons.

Ryan grinned when he saw me. “Wasn’t that great?”

Outrunning the police was amazing in an unreal, impossible kind of way. But I wasn’t going to tell Ryan that. “It was stupid. I told you we would get in trouble and we did.” I stuck my feet into my shoes without untying them.

“Did not.”

“Yes we did.” I crawled out of the tent. We were almost nose-to-nose. “I call having the police chase us getting in trouble.”

“Only counts if you get caught.” He smirked.

GREAT OAKS ~~SCHOOL~~ PRISON

I wake up on a mattress on the floor of an empty room. Someone is screaming in the night, but it's not the fighting voices that usually wake me. One lone voice howls for help. Someone's pounding on his door like he's trying to break it down.

I know it isn't a dream. I slip off to sleep and dream I'm the one pounding on locked doors, and each door opens into another empty room where I am trapped again.

Someone pulls me up by my shoulders. Water rolls down my chin.

Big Nose says, "Drink, Robbie."

My head feels like a giant is squeezing it. Big Nose shines a bright light in each of my eyes. It is like being stabbed in the eye with an orange marker. Orange dots blink at me from every direction.

"He looks good," says Big Nose.

"Is this what you wanted? To stay here forever?" Mr. Lester's voice is a low growl.

"Food," I groan.

Mr. Lester sets a paper plate on the floor next to my bed. Two pieces of toast.

"I'm hurt. Can I have food? Or apple juice? Please?"

"You get this," says Mr. Lester. He puts a piece of paper and a pencil on the floor. "Take responsibility, Robbie. Make me a list of how you got into this mess. Then we'll both figure out a way to get you out."

There's a way out?

When Mr. Lester opens the door to leave, a voice calls down the hall, "Somebody?"

RIVER FALLS

The first day of seventh grade was like the first day of every grade. Everyone was wearing new clothes and wishing it were still summer. Anna Beth Carter bounced over to me. She had ribbons woven into her tiny braids and flicked her head back and forth to snap them. “Our summer soccer team went undefeated.”

I backed away before she could slap me in the face with her hair. “I’ll sit in the back.”

Ryan came in just before the bell. He slid into the seat next to me wearing dirty jeans and a crumpled shirt. He smelled like oranges.

Mr. Michaels marched into the classroom and stood behind his desk. He lifted a stack of books in the air and let them drop—Bang! We all jumped. He said, “Now that I have your attention, everyone up, out of your seats. Form a line in the back of the room.”

We stood and started to move.

He added, “Take your belongings with you. You won’t be allowed to choose your seat in my class, boys and girls.”

Anna Beth Carter raised her hand. “Mr. Michaels, how should we line up?”

“In a single line.”

She flicked her braids behind her shoulders and squinted. “I mean, by age, or height, or birthday, or something?”

He put his hands on his hips and stalked halfway across the

room. “I mean in one line in the back!” He leaned against a desk. “I haven’t been a teacher for twenty-two and a half years without learning a thing or two.” He pulled the class list out of his pocket and walked in front of the line looking at each one of us. “I know how to spot the troublemakers on the first day of school without even looking at you.”

Mr. Michaels walked to the whiteboard. “Looks like there are just two problem children in our class. Only two.” He pulled the cap off a red marker and wrote: *Anna Beth Carter.* “Troublemaker number one, ABC. Sit right here, front and center.”

Anna Beth’s face was complete shock. She looked like she was going to cry. “Not me. Not me! Check the record. I’m a top student. I get the best grades. I’m on the honor roll. Ask anyone.”

“Starting trouble already,” Mr. Michaels said. “Get to the front.”

He lifted his hand again and we all held our breath. If Anna Beth Carter was considered a troublemaker, it could be any one of the rest of us.

He wrote: Robert Sander Thompson.

“RST, get here and share a table with ABC.”

I didn’t talk back. I sat down next to Anna Beth.

How could I be a troublemaker?

Mr. Michaels stood in front of me and Anna Beth. He made his voice loud enough for the entire class to hear. “It’s your parents’ fault. Naming you with your little alphabet names all in a row. It’s been the case every year in every class I ever taught. These kids are trouble with a capital T. Your parents think you’re cute, don’t they? They spoil you and you come to school with an attitude!” He imitated Anna Beth. “I’m a top student.” Mr. Michaels looked around the room. Everyone was listening. “The rest of the class suffers. The teacher suffers. Well, not in my classroom, ABC. Not in my classroom, RST.”

I hadn’t done anything! My eyes stung like I’d been walking in a snowstorm.

Mr. Michaels didn't talk to me or Anna Beth the rest of the day. I didn't listen to a thing he said, but I could tell he was nice to the other kids. As soon as the bell rang, I ran out of that room and out the front door. A few minutes later Ryan was behind me.

"I brought your backpack," he said. "And your jacket."

"I hate that guy. I hate him." My fists tightened. I wanted to punch something, someone—Mr. Michaels—but there was nothing I could do.

We waited for the light on Main Street.

Ryan said, "Come on, let's take the long way home." He wanted to walk by the construction site. We snuck up near the back, between the trees and the fence. The cranes were lifting and swinging. A bulldozer sat still by the corner of the fence. It had black writing on the side. I walked over for a closer look. *Ryan was here* was spelled out with black spray paint.

"Are you crazy?" I asked him. "You wrote your name?"

Ryan smiled like one of my mom's daycare kids showing off a paper with scribbles on it. "Isn't it great?"

"No! It's stupid! You're here all day, every day. You try to sneak in during the day. You break in at night. Then you write your name!!! They're going to find out."

"What do you care?"

I sat down on the ground. I didn't care. A teacher hated me, thought I was a troublemaker, and he didn't even know me. I started to cry.

"What the hell are you doing?" Ryan asked. "What the hell is it with the water faucet? Turn it off."

The more he yelled, the more I cried.

"Why are you acting like a baby? You only get to cry until you're two years old. You are not allowed to cry, hear me?"

"I hate him!"

Ryan tackled me and sat on my chest. "Who cares? Who cares about him?"

"He doesn't even know me and he hates me."

He punched me on the shoulder. "Who cares?"

I cried. He hit me again.

"*No* one likes *me*," said Ryan between punches. "You don't cry about *me*!"

"Stop, stop!" I tried to hit him back, but every time I threw a punch he leaned away. He hit my chest, my shoulders, even my jaw. He seemed to time his punches to land right when I wanted to take a breath. I couldn't cry or even breathe. His fists pounded into my chest and choked me.

He rolled off. "I didn't mean to beat you so hard." He was panting. "I just can't stand to hear a stinking baby crying. Crying, crying, crying. Like a stupid baby."

I sat up. "You freak!" I jumped on him. I hit him, but I was still crying.

He rolled me over like I was nothing and stood up. "You are the freak, Robbie." He kicked gravel at me. "You have everything. Big fancy house. Food anytime you want it. A whole room full of crap. Your dad's not dead. And you cry because some teacher is a jerk. So what!?" He sprayed me again with gravel. "I'm so sick of you. I hate you. I hate the flowers on your table and the stupid plates for every meal."

I was on my feet in an instant, ready to push him, to punch him. *Plates?* I wanted to run at him, but I knew he'd just start hitting again. "You're not sick of the food! You show up for meals and clean your stupid plate just fine, don't you?"

"Let's see you eat at my house for a change. Oh wait, you're afraid of a house."

I wasn't afraid at that moment. I wasn't afraid at all. I was going to tell him, but then someone started crying and it wasn't me.

GREAT OAKS ~~SCHOOL~~ PRISON

I can think of only one strategy. Admit to everything.

Responsibility

1. I killed Ryan.
2. I beat up kids at Red Brick, guys who used to be my friends.
3. I got into fights at Superintendent's School. Mostly I was defending myself, but not always.
4. I threw a chair out the window at the International School.
5. I destroyed my room at St. Christopher's.
6. I smashed my chair and wrote on my door here.
7. I don't want to talk in group. I don't want to talk about what happened.

I crawl out of bed and slide the paper under the door. When I wake up, there is a sub sandwich, potato chips, and three paper cups of apple juice next to my bed.

RIVER FALLS

A real baby was screaming his head off. Ryan walked up the hill to the boarded-up mini-market. There was a lady in a baggy sweat suit staring at a tiny baby on her lap.

Ryan sat down next to her and reached out and touched the baby's head. "Is she yours?"

"He's a boy. Course he's mine." She scowled at Ryan.

"What's her name?" Ryan asked.

"A boy. Wynn."

Wynn's face was red and his mouth was open wide, crying. Tears rolled down his cheeks. The lady just looked at him. "I used to live here," she said. "I thought this place would be open."

"Is she wet?" Ryan asked. "Did you change her diaper?"

"He's dry."

"You need to change the diaper every time it gets wet. Don't try to save diapers to save money, because she could get an infection." Ryan sounded like he was reading a book.

"He's a boy!" The lady raised her voice. Wynn cried louder.

"Well, is she hungry?"

The lady looked up at Ryan, then over at me. "He won't take a bottle." She held Wynn out in front of her and swayed him back and forth a little and set him down on the bench, laying him on his back. "I can't make him stop crying."

Ryan reached out and took the baby, just like it was someone he knew. Just like he'd been holding babies his whole life.

He stood up and started walking around patting the little guy's back. Wynn still cried, but softer now.

"That's it," said Ryan. He sang *Twinkle, Twinkle Little Star* soft and low.

"He's really good with kids," I said. But the lady wasn't worried about Wynn. She wasn't watching him or listening to me. She was staring at the boarded-up door of the grocery store as if looking at it could make it open back up again.

I leaned against the wall and watched Ryan pace. His steps matched the tune of the song. After Ryan sang the song three times, Wynn stopped crying. Ryan sat down next to the lady. "She had some gas, burped twice."

Wynn started to whimper. "Maybe she'll eat now?" Ryan asked.

The lady didn't tell him again that Wynn was a boy. She just nodded to the bottle sticking out of the baby's bag. Ryan rested Wynn back and gave him the bottle. He drank every last drop. Ryan lifted Wynn up to his shoulder and patted Wynn's back until he burped again.

"There you go," he said. He handed Wynn back to his mother.

"Thanks, kid," she whispered.

We walked away from the construction site. "Where did you learn to do that?" I asked. "My mom's had a daycare since I was two and I don't know any of that."

"I used to have—I mean, I have—a sister. Her name's Star. I don't even know where she is."

"When did you see her last? Did she come with you to your grandparents' house?"

Ryan marched forward in silence, ignoring my questions like he did the first day we met. He stopped when we got to Howell Street.

"Just answer me, would you?" I asked.

"I don't want to talk about it," Ryan said. He turned to go.

"Stop. I'm not afraid. I'll come to your house."

Ryan looked me up and down. "Leave me alone," he said. He sprinted away.

GREAT OAKS ~~SCHOOL~~ PRISON

Mr. Lester comes in and sits cross-legged on the floor. "Do you remember what happened in group?"

"My chair tipped back, I fell."

"And before that?"

"Fighting with The Beef."

Mr. Lester heaves himself up and paces around my bed. "You deliberately provoked an attack. Did you come here to keep screwing up? To get hurt? You want to try the same kind of games here that you played everywhere else? Is that it?"

"No."

"Well what is it, Robbie? Because I don't know. Where's the kid who told me he wanted to figure things out? The boy who wanted to get back home?"

"I want to go home. I want to." My eyes sting. I'm afraid he's going to make me start over, back at square one. "I'll do anything, really."

Mr. Lester gives me my list back. He says, "Tomorrow we'll figure out what to do next."

I can't sleep, not because I slept too much during the day, but because I finally figure out who it is pounding on the door down the hall and crying for help. The Beef.

RIVER FALLS

Ryan started avoiding me after our fight. But he was taking my advice from last year and pretending to be a normal kid. He raised his hand, answered questions, and talked to everyone.

I learned names of the kids at Mom's daycare and memorized jokes to tell them so they wouldn't miss Ryan too much. I even colored with them. Still, they wanted me to walk on my hands, and Ryan was the only one I knew who could do something like that.

> To: Robbie Thompson
> From: Grant Reynolds
> Hey. I'm burning up here in the desert. It's so hot I have to drink water all the time. My skin would boil if I didn't. I wear a big canteen, called a camel back, on my back. Water's good and plenty of it, so it's all good! See you later!

Another stupid e-mail. Pretending to like the desert. Grown-ups always say "it's all good" when nothing is good at all.

I told Mom the same thing about school. "Everything's fine." But it wasn't. Mr. Michaels hated me. He asked me questions like, "RST, what item on the food pyramid is not a food?"

I thought it was a trick question. We studied the food pyramid two years ago. "All items of the food pyramid are foods," I said, and named them all.

"Incorrect," said Mr. Michaels. "Physical activity is a daily part of the food pyramid. Your list is old news. Keep up with the times, RST."

Then he made jokes about my answers all day long. We had a math bee at the end of the morning. Everyone else got to answer easy questions and mine were triple hard. But I showed him. I got every answer right and won the entire thing. Mr. Michaels didn't say "A round of applause for the winner, please" like he did when other students won. As far as he was concerned, I was invisible. Anna Beth Carter was invisible. And every other kid in class was normal, even Ryan. Instead of asking for applause, Mr. Michaels said, "Good thing for you this math doesn't get updated once in a while like the food pyramid."

After lunch Mr. Michaels started again. "RST, spell 'Constantinople.' "

I had no idea. "You mean the old way or the new updated version?"

The kids laughed. Mr. Michaels' veins stood out on his neck. He leaned over my desk until his face was close to mine. His fish breath covered my face. "That is quite enough! Maybe you think school is a comedy show. But the other students come here to learn, and it's my responsibility to make sure they do just that!"

I couldn't breathe. My eyes burned. When he stood up I couldn't even blink. I was afraid water would roll down my cheek.

Anna Beth reached her hand under the table and rested it on my leg.

I leaned close to her and whispered in her ear, "Get your hand off me!"

She jerked her hand away and scribbled a note on a scrap of paper.

> *I'm sorry. It just looked like you were going to cry. I wanted to be a friend.*

I tore the paper up into tiny pieces. I couldn't let her, or anyone, think that I'd actually cry at school. I took out my own paper and wrote:

> *Mr. Michaels screamed in my face with onion breath. It stung my eyes. Upset my stomach too. I think I'm going to barf up my lunch. Is barf on the new food pyramid???*

Anna Beth read my note and gave a tiny, very soft half giggle.

"Something funny over there?" Mr. Michaels eyed us.

"No, no." Anna Beth tucked my note under her paper.

Mr. Michaels made a dive for it like a linebacker trying to recover a fumble. He held up the folded square of paper. "What do we have here?" He smiled. He scored a touchdown.

When Mr. Michaels discovered a student passing a note, he read the note to the whole class. Why did I think I could get away with it? I knew I'd get in big trouble, but to hear him read about his own stinky breath would be worth any punishment. The class jiggled in their seats like a theater full of people with the screen about to change from advertisements to previews. Mr. Michaels sat down at his desk and scribbled something on a piece of paper. He didn't read my note to the class. Instead he handed one to me:

> *No recess—1 week.*
> *500 word essay "I respect my teacher"*
> *You will give a speech to the class about the new food pyramid.*

After school, Mom asked me a dozen times, "What's wrong?"

I answered, "Everything's fine." Until I got sick of the question and said, "I don't want to talk about it."

Before bed, she came into my room. "I'll do the talking. Anna Beth's mom called. She said that you got in some kind of trouble today."

"Anna Beth! You're going to believe her over me?"

Mom sat down in my desk chair and twisted it around, facing me. "And Ryan hasn't been here in two weeks."

"Ryan is a jerk. He..." I almost told her that he tried to beat me up. But I didn't want her to know that a shrimp like Ryan could pound her son. "He's bad news."

Mom looked at my carpet. I watched the fish on the screen saver behind her.

"Mom. Everything's fine."

"Okay." She ruffled my hair and left, pulling my door closed. She poked her head back in. "If you want to talk, I'm here."

I couldn't sleep. It wasn't the speech, missing recess, or the disgusting essay. *I respect my teacher.* I'd have to lie to write it, but what choice did I have? For the first time in my life I hated school. I hated everything. Mom was watching TV. She clicked it off fast when she saw me. I sat down next to her and started talking before I changed my mind. "Mom, what do you do when you feel sad?"

She kissed the top of my head, pulled me up, and took me to the kitchen. She got us each a bowl of chocolate-marshmallow ice cream. Still she didn't talk. I was beginning to think that she hadn't heard my question.

She cleared her throat and said, "When I'm sad, there're only two things I know to do. I'm not sure if either one will help you."

"What's number one?"

Mom filled her spoon and said, "You're eating it."

"Chocolate-marshmallow ice cream? That's your advice?"

Mom smiled. "It can be any flavor, whatever you like best. Good thing I'm not sad often or I'd weigh a ton."

I started to lose hope. I liked ice cream, but I didn't expect it could actually help me with anything. "What's number two?"

"Number two is not easy, but it's worth it. You have to really think, look around you, or go off and discover it. But you must find someone who is even sadder than you are and help them feel better."

Just what I needed. That would be even more difficult than writing about respecting my teacher. I mashed my ice cream with my spoon until it was in between solid and liquid and drank it from my bowl. "Thanks, Mom."

I thought of everyone I knew. Sure, there were people who had worse problems than a mean teacher. I logged on to my account and sent Uncle Grant a great e-mail. I included a bunch of jokes from my "joke a day" folder and attached a few silly pictures. I wrote about how great life was in River Falls. I signed it "See you later."

Mom's advice had started to work. I was almost asleep when I thought about Ryan and his baby sister, Star. Somewhere in the world, in the U.S. probably, maybe even Ohio, was his baby sister. He missed her. He could really take care of her. He knew all about diapers and feeding, even burping.

I fell asleep with Mom's words in my ears: "Find someone who is even sadder than you are and do what you can to help them."

GREAT OAKS ~~SCHOOL~~ PRISON

Sleep is impossible. My body aches. I can feel the floor through my mattress, feel the bruises growing on my hips and shoulders from lying here too long. Even empty, the room is tiny.

I run a lap around the room, slap the door "One" and run another lap. "Two." I'm tired before I say twenty but keep going until I've run twenty-five times. I wake up throughout the night and run until I can sleep again.

It must be morning. My legs ache and my chest feels tight but I doubt I even ran a mile last night. Each sit-up is agony on my bruised back. I only manage nine. I roll over and start on push-ups, counting my progress each time my elbows straighten.

"Eighteen, nineteen, twenty—"

A cough tells me I'm being watched. Mr. Lester claps his hands slowly and lets a piece of paper fall to the floor. "I've made the list this time. You've got work to do today. Earl will bring you supplies after breakfast."

RIVER FALLS

The next day before school, I tried to talk to Ryan. "Hey," I said. He walked right past me. I tried to catch up with him when the class zoomed out the door to recess. Mr. Michaels grabbed my shoulder. "No recess for you, RST."

I found him at the construction site after school. There was a big hole in the ground now; all of the machines were inside it. I leaned up against the fence next to Ryan and wondered how they got those huge machines down there.

"What are you doing here?" Ryan asked.

"Just looking." A huge yellow sign read: COMING SOON! SPORTS TROPOLIS!

"Sports Tropolis! They're building a Sports Tropolis!"

"So you can read," said Ryan. "Big deal."

"Sports Tropolis! Have you ever been to one?"

"When they build it, this will be gone." Ryan would miss the construction site, like a preschooler and his first sandbox.

"Sports Tropolis is only the coolest sports store in the world. You don't just try stuff on, you try it out. Haven't you seen their commercials? They have a climbing wall. A huge trampoline. You can put on in-lines and skate, right in the store. For free."

Ryan looked at me like I was speaking another language. "So what?"

He walked away.

"Hey Ryan," I hollered. "I'm not afraid of your house, you know. I can eat there."

He stopped and let me catch up. "You serious?"

"Sure, anytime."

"In that case, turn around."

Ryan led me to Paradise Foods. Instead of going into the store, he started walking along the entire edge of the parking lot. "Look for bottles," he said. "Cans, too."

When we had eight bottles we went into the store and fed them into the monster machine. We traded our trash for cash. Well, a piece of paper that we could use for cash.

Ryan led me down aisle six, pasta and international foods. He picked up a plain white box. Macaroni and cheese.

"Oh, cool. I like mac 'n cheese." But Ryan grabbed the yuck box, the kind with clumpy cheese and hard noodles.

I pointed to a different brand. "Let's get this one, the ones cut into shapes, moons and stars and stuff."

Ryan just stomped away. He was quiet the entire walk home.

"Why didn't we get the good macaroni and cheese?"

We were at the corner of Pine, only a few blocks from Ryan's house.

"Compare prices, brainiac. I bet you never had to compare prices in your life."

"I could have paid. I have some money, I think." I put my hand in my pocket and pulled out a wadded-up ten and two ones.

"You didn't even know if you had money or not?" Ryan looked back in the direction of Paradise Foods. "You idiot. We could have got something good."

I tried to change the subject. "Why don't you ever talk about your mom or your sister?"

"Why don't you ever talk about your uncle when he's not around?"

"Does your sister live with your mom?"

Ryan stopped walking. "I told you, my mom is in the hospital. Do you think they'd let a baby stay in a hospital if she's not sick?"

"I don't know. Why didn't she come with you?"

"They said this place wasn't fit for babies." Ryan turned up the path to his grandparents' house. We were at 111 Howell Street and I didn't even have time to be afraid. I scanned the porch, no Grandpa. Ryan walked carefully up the steps, putting his feet on the outside edges. When I got close, I discovered why: huge holes, rotten wood in the middle of every step.

I followed him in. It was so dark inside, my eyes had to adjust. When they did, I couldn't believe it. It really was like a haunted house. Huge cobwebs hung in every corner. The old furniture was covered in two layers—a layer of plastic and a layer of dust. The walls were so dirty they were gray with black smears. With every breath I could smell cat crap.

Ryan was gone. I heard running water and followed my ears. Ryan stood at a big sink in the kitchen rinsing out a white bowl with orange dots inside it.

An old lady called from down the hall. "Boy, that you? Boy?"

Ryan answered, "Yeah."

"Where's my mush?!"

Ryan pulled a slice of bread out of a bag. "Coming!"

He balanced the bread on one hand, sprinkled water on top, and rubbed it in. He turned the bread over and did it again.

"What are you doing?"

"Making the bread soft."

I touched a piece of dry bread. It was hard and spongy like an eraser.

Ryan poured the cheese powder into the bowl. Then he added a little water and mixed it with his fingers. More water. More mixing. I noticed that the orange spots on the sides of the bowl were dried cheese mix from the last time. Or the time before that. Or the time before that.

The old lady's voice called again. "Boy? Where'd you go?"

"Coming!" Ryan hollered at the top of his lungs. He scooped some of the cheese mixture into a coffee cup, ripped the moist bread, and put it on top.

"I gotta take her something to eat or she'd just keep yelling."

I watched him go.

Ryan returned before I had time for another thought. I didn't have time to think of what we were going to eat. He took two more coffee cups and plopped the rest of the cheese guck inside. He watered another piece of bread. I figured it was more "mush" for his grandmother.

He looked up at me and said, "Aren't you going to get some bread?"

"Oh, bread. Sure, I'll help. How much water does she need on each side?"

He set a coffee cup in front of me. "She has her dinner. Bread. For you."

"Dinner? This? I mean...aren't you going to cook the noodles?"

Ryan was joking, paying me back. He couldn't be serious, could he?

"I thought you weren't afraid."

"I'm not." I really wasn't. I was disgusted, not afraid. I played along, sprinkled water on my bread and waited for Ryan to tell me he was joking.

The water did make the bread softer. I flipped my bread over.

Ryan reached his fingers down into the coffee cup and scooped up the orange slime. He smeared it over his bread.

I pretended not to notice and watched him out of the corner of my eye. He actually folded the bread in half and took a bite, like it was a regular sandwich.

My stomach clenched. Ugh! How could he eat that?

"Thought you wanted to eat dinner with me." He had a poker face.

I checked my bread for mold, stuck a corner into the cheese slime, and waited for him to say "Tricked you!" I watched Ryan eat the rest of his sandwich and realized it wasn't a joke. He wouldn't eat that much himself if it weren't for real.

I took a small bite and felt a goo ball in my mouth. I knew it was just old bread and yuck cheese powder, but I gagged. All I could smell was cat dung. All I could see was filth.

Ryan stared at me. He took the bread out of my hand, covered it with the rest of the cheese mix and held it under my nose. "Take a big bite."

"I'm not hungry."

"I dare you."

I took a bite. My entire mouth gagged. I ran to the porch, jumped over all four steps, leaned into the bushes and barfed.

GREAT OAKS ~~SCHOOL~~ PRISON

Slivers of paint stab under my fingernails, my fingertips are bleeding, and my elbows ache, but I'm not going to stop sanding until the door is smooth. I have to prove to Mr. Lester that I can be trusted with furniture if I move upstairs; I am fixing what I've destroyed.

I sand all morning and begin painting in the afternoon. Mr. Lester comes to check on my door at dinnertime. I am exhausted but happy. The H E L P that I had carved has been sanded away.

"Do you like it? Can I move upstairs tonight?"

"Let's give it one more coat of paint in the morning, just to be sure."

My last night in the torture chamber. No matter what happens, I won't end up back here. I am on my way up—to TV, Ping-Pong, phone calls, visitors, and a whole big cafeteria full of food.

In the morning, Earl brings the paint and brush in with my breakfast tray. "Heard you might be moving on upstairs today?"

"I hope so." It feels odd, Earl just starting up a conversation with me, like I'm a regular person.

"I'm glad for ya," he says. "Glad to see you finally gettin' out. That other kid is in a world of hurt." He jerks his thumb at my wall in the direction of the screams. I'm so used to the noise now I don't really hear it anymore. "Some kids can take it here, some can't."

After painting, I sit on my mattress and watch the paint dry.

It feels like someone else's room already. Without my things, the clock, calendar, and my letters, there is nothing here that belongs to me. I have only a couple pieces of paper and a pencil.

I know what Mr. Lester wants me to write next, a plan to go home. But I don't have one single idea.

RIVER FALLS

There is a tiny bit of time when our house is actually quiet. It's after the last kid is picked up from daycare and before Dad comes home for dinner. A few minutes after the last kid left, the door burst open and someone called for Mom.

I sat on the top of the stairs and watched Christy, Uncle Grant's fiancée, fly back and forth between the living room and the kitchen. "Is anyone here?" I stood up and was about to say something when Mom ran past me and down the stairs.

"What's wrong?" Mom asked, and hugged her. I'd never seen anyone in our family hug Christy before, except Uncle Grant. Mom led Christy to the sofa and told her to sit down. I crept to the middle of the stairs and peeked over the rail. Christy didn't sit. She walked from one end of the room to the other.

"What's wrong?! Tell me!"

Christy shook her head.

Mom started a guessing game. "Are you pregnant?"

"God, no!" said Christy.

"You two breaking up again?"

Christy rolled her head side to side and said, "No," real soft.

Then Mom sat down, her voice deep and low. "Grant's hurt."

"He called me." Christie took a deep breath. "He's going into surgery. He said, 'Tell my mom not to panic, she'll probably get a call pretty soon.' "

"Hurt where?"

"He didn't tell me. He said, 'Whatever I've lost, I haven't lost my mind.' He couldn't hear me talking to him." She choked out a sob. "His voice was so loud, but he couldn't hear me."

Christy stopped talking and started crying. Mom sank deeper into the sofa, put her elbows on her knees and her forehead in her hands. She looked bent in half.

I ran to check my e-mail. If Uncle Grant was able to call Christy, he might have had time to send me a message. My inbox was empty. Even though Dad had told me not to, I opened up the Internet and did a search for Tikrit. There was a car explosion five weeks ago, but nothing reported since then.

"This is stupid," I said to my computer. Really, what good was the Internet when it didn't have the information you needed?

Mom drove Christy to Grandma's and told me to stay close to the phone.

I was leaning against the wall in the kitchen staring at the phone when Dad came home from work. Mom wasn't back yet. As soon as he walked into the kitchen, I said, "Grant's hurt. I'm waiting in case there is a phone call."

He took out his cell phone. "I'll call your mom."

"Don't. They're all waiting. If she gets a call, she'll think it's about . . ."

Instead he used his phone to order pizza, and Mom was home before it was delivered. We stayed up all night waiting for news. Mom and I tried to do jigsaw puzzles. Dad put in a few movies, but really we just listened for the phone. It didn't ring.

I fell asleep on the sofa and woke up at 5 A.M. My face had lines from the cushions and my cheek was covered with drool slime.

"I'm too tired for school," I told Mom.

I thought she'd make me go anyway, but she nodded and said, "Yeah."

Grandma called at 10:30 in the morning. Mom hung up and held the phone to her like a girl holding a teddy bear. "It's like we've been waiting for this call for so long and we know nothing more than we did before. Grant underwent 'unspecified surgeries' and has 'unknown injuries.' He's being flown to Germany for 'immediate care.' "

"What?"

"It means the person who called Grandma didn't get told a whole heck of a lot," Dad said. "Uncle Grant is hurt, bad enough to leave the job. He's going to a bigger, better hospital where they'll take good care of him."

I had a million questions. How did he get hurt? Why did he need surgery? Where was he hurt? Why was he going to Germany instead of the U.S.? How long until he came home?

I didn't ask a single question. No one I knew had the answers.

Later that day, we found out that Uncle Grant had injuries to his "upper and lower extremities," medical talk for arms and legs.

"Broken bones?" I asked.

"We don't know," Mom said.

"Will he get to come home?"

Mom sighed. "I don't know."

Grandma and Christy decided to fly to Germany. They couldn't even sit next to each other at the dinner table. Now they were flying on the same plane and sharing a room. I felt even sorrier for Uncle Grant.

When Ryan came over that night, I told him.

He said, "That sucks. But it's kinda cool, too."

I wanted to sink my fists into him! How could he even say that?

"Not that he's hurt. I mean cool he'll come back. We'll get to see him."

Actually, I'd been thinking that, too. Ryan pushed back his hair and rubbed his hands together. "And he can tell us about being in a real war."

I walked away from him so I wouldn't punch him in the face.

GREAT OAKS ~~SCHOOL~~ PRISON

The Beef's cries turn into croaks, like his voice is wearing out. I scratch his name on the top of the paper.

The Beef—

I have been through it all here in Great Oaks' torture chamber. I can help him a little. I write: *When it's time to write your lists, do your very best. Write everything (except commentary) and tell the truth.*

There has to be something more I can tell him, something that will give him hope. I add: *And remember when you write your "I want" list, don't forget to include "I want to go home" and "I want my door unlocked so I can use the bathroom."*

Mr. Lester shows up with my stuff in a box. "You carry this. I'm not a transportation service."

I trail slowly behind Mr. Lester as we walk down the hall. When I'm sure that I'm outside The Beef's door, I set the box down and quickly slip the note underneath.

RIVER FALLS

Two days after we found out Uncle Grant was hurt I couldn't concentrate in school. I hardly noticed Mr. Michaels at all until he pounded a fist on my desk.

"RST, where is your brain today?"

"I'm thinking about my uncle. He was wounded in Iraq."

He squatted down in front of me and whispered, "Stay here after school." He didn't call on me the rest of the day. At least I don't think he did.

After school I walked up to his desk. "I know you hate me and everything. I'm not trying to cause trouble. It's just that my uncle's hurt and we don't know anything..."

Mr. Michaels actually smiled at me. "Come on, Robbie. I don't hate you. I'm really sorry about your uncle. My thoughts are with you and your family."

I couldn't believe it. He was being nice—to me! "Now, if you need to talk about this, come to me after class. But don't mention this war business during school hours. It's disruptive. We need a calm environment for learning. You understand that, right?" Same old Mr. Michaels, he really didn't want me to talk to him. He just wanted me quiet during class.

"Right." I left as fast as possible.

Ms. Lacey would have cared. She would have explained about extremities to the whole class. I went to my old classroom.

There was a kid there working on an assignment. "Ms. Lacey's in the library," he said.

I found Ms. Lacey with Mrs. Bird, our librarian. I told them about Uncle Grant. Ms. Lacey wrapped her arms around me. "I don't care if you think you're too big for a hug. This is one of those times you just need one. Either you need to get one or I need to give one." I didn't mind the hug. Mrs. Bird bent over and hugged me, too.

When I got home, Mom told me another medical word. Amputation. Amputation means part of an extremity being cut off. That's what happened to Uncle Grant. Amputation. Amputa*tions* really, two of them. Left arm. Left leg.

I went for a run. I thought about Uncle Grant. All the runs we've been on. Everything he ever taught me. I wouldn't even be a runner if it weren't for him. At home I dug in Mom's desk for a permanent marker and found one of my white T-shirts to wear to my next race. I wrote on it in big block letters:

I SUPPORT MY UNCLE WHO WAS WOUNDED IN IRAQ.

GREAT OAKS ~~SCHOOL~~ PRISON

"Can I get another pair of slippers?" Mine are covered in brown dots from the paint and they're starting to tear.

"How long are you going to keep wearing those things?"

"Until I get my socks and shoes."

Mr. Lester laughs. He opens the supply closet and tosses a few slipper packets into my box. We walk past our group room to a circular desk and three red doors. Mr. Lester pushes a button by one of the doors and says, "It's me, Lester. With Robbie."

The door buzzes and we step into a sort of fake house, a big open room with a TV in one corner and a sofa and chairs around it. Books are in another corner and a wobbly Ping-Pong table stands in the middle of the room. Across from me, five beds are lined up against the wall. Three of the beds have signs above them.

Over the bed on the left:

Vincent Spinoza
Level: 4 Tokens: 196

Over the bed on the right:

Curtis Rodgers
Level: 4 Tokens: 2,654

In the very center is my bed:

Robert Thompson
Level: 2 Tokens: -114

"Why am I only at level two? Why don't I have any tokens?"

"Tokens were deducted to account for your damage to our property."

"Yeah, but I just spent two days fixing that door."

Mr. Lester nods. "Yes, we calculated that. The remaining negative balance is for the chair. Now hurry up or you'll miss lunch."

RIVER FALLS

When I came down for breakfast I wore a sweatshirt over the T-shirt I made.

"Are you sure you're up for a race, today?" Mom pulled me into a hug. "You don't have to. We've all been through so much."

"I want to run. Uncle Grant would want me to run."

I started the race smooth and fast. One foot in front of the other. I couldn't stop myself from thinking of what it would be like to have an amputation. A whole arm missing. A leg. A foot. Gone. The middle parts—elbows and knees—were somehow important now. Mom and Dad had been telling everyone, "The leg was amputated above the knee, but he still has his elbow and most of his arm."

Stupid grown-up talk. Uncle Grant didn't have a foot and his whole hand was missing. Elbows? Knees? That's just extra.

Grandma had been calling us from Germany every night. I begged to talk to Uncle Grant. She always said the same thing, "He's in his room. I'm in the lobby. I'll tell him what you want to say." But I didn't have anything to say. I just wanted to hear his voice, make sure it was still the same. Make sure *he* was still the same.

I pulled off my sweatshirt and tied it around my neck. Then I remembered the T-shirt I made, and put the sweatshirt around my waist. A few people ran past and gave me the thumbs-up.

A lady ran with me and told me that her son was in Iraq. She wanted to know Uncle Grant's unit and everything. I told her all I knew. He's in the reserves. He was in Tikrit.

This guy with wild hair ran up beside me. He got all excited talking about Uncle Grant. "It's a crime what happened to that boy. A crime. They need to stop this war and bring the boys home. Bring them home. That's what I say."

I didn't answer. Uncle Grant was coming home. I thought about him all the time, but I didn't think much about the other people over there, the Americans or the people who lived there. I tried not to think about the war.

Crazy Hair didn't let up. "Are you running in protest? If you're running in protest, I'm with you."

I don't like to talk when I run. But Crazy Hair started running backward in front of me and slowing me down. My shirt said I was running in support of my uncle. Support is not a protest. "I'm just running for my uncle. I want him to be okay."

"A-men," the guy said, and turned around and ran off.

I grabbed water at every stand after that, oranges, too. My legs turned into jelly. It hurt to breathe. But I didn't stop. I was covered in so much sweat it was like I'd been out in a thunderstorm. But I finished.

A bunch of kids from school were there. Ryan had done it again.

"Robbie." Mom hugged me, even though I was sweaty. "I had no idea you were...that you would run for..." She stopped and caught her breath. "Such a long race. Wow."

Ryan held his hand up and I slapped it. "Pretty cool, runner guy," he said.

"Yeah, pretty cool." I worked my way down the line of hands: Tyler, Dylan, Everett, Colin, Elsa, and Anna Beth Carter. I stopped, looked up, and slapped another hand.

It was my dad's.

GREAT OAKS ~~SCHOOL~~ PRISON

There are about fifty older kids in the cafeteria and they start jabbering as soon as we open the door. "He's here! That's him! There he is!" They stare and point at me, and laugh at my slippers. I have to walk in front of everyone to get to the food counter. I move across the room as fast as I can without running. When everyone is behind me, it's easy to ignore them. When I'm finally holding a tray full of food at the end of the line, I turn and realize I'll have to sit somewhere.

"Over here, little firecracker," 76 calls. He's sitting with Big in the back of the room.

I lock my eyes on the empty spot at their table and speed over there. Only after I'm seated do I take a good long look at my food. So much food: meatloaf, potatoes, salad, corn, carrot sticks, and applesauce. "I can't believe we get all this food."

76 points to the food line with his fork. "If you eat it all, you can go back one more time for seconds."

Seconds! "No way."

"It's true," Big says. He smiles. "Welcome to paradise."

RIVER FALLS

Grandma phoned with good news. Uncle Grant was well enough go to a hospital in the USA, in Washington, D.C. A few days later, Mom closed her daycare and left me and Dad alone for a week to visit Uncle Grant.

The day she left, a huge box was delivered to our door, addressed to me from Uncle Grant. The box took up half the dining table. I could have stuck ten basketballs inside without even having to shove. The packing slip said the box contained "handcrafted travel supplies."

"What do you think it is?" I asked.

Dad lifted the box to the floor and handed me the kitchen scissors. "Open it."

I slid the scissors over the top, cut down the sides and pulled out a lump covered in brown paper. Underneath was a curved piece of wood with long, sparkly ropes hanging over the sides. Dad turned it round and round. "It's some sort of small table. Or a chair."

I tore open the envelope.

Hey Robbie,

I have no idea what you'll do with this, but you are now the owner of a genuine handmade camel saddle.

Pretty cool, eh? Maybe your dad'll buy you a camel and you can ride it to school.

I see a bunch of camels every day, but most of them aren't wearing saddles. Here's a picture of me standing by a Black Hawk. Huge, ain't it?

Thanks for the e-mails. Send more pictures and more jokes.

Love,

Uncle Grant

"It's a camel saddle," I told Dad. I pulled the photo out of the envelope. Uncle Grant stood in front of a gigantic helicopter. He smiled big. He still had two arms and two legs. I looked at his left arm and leg in the photo and tried to imagine Uncle Grant without them. I passed the photo to Dad and carried my saddle up to my room.

GREAT OAKS ~~SCHOOL~~ PRISON

Being on the fifth floor is worthless, since I have no tokens. I can't watch TV because it costs ten tokens for half an hour. I can't use the phone (ten tokens per call). I can't even play Ping-Pong (three tokens from each player).

There is a rule against loaning, borrowing, or selling tokens. It's impossible anyway because the tokens aren't real things. They're not coins or poker chips that you can hold in your hand and trade around. They're just a number in the computer (controlled by the green-coverall guys) and scribbled on the boards above our beds. If I'm lucky enough to "achieve my goals" I can earn ten tokens a day.

Sleeping in the same room with people is strange. Big tosses and turns in his sleep, 76 doesn't snore exactly, but his nose whistles. And there is always someone who works at Great Oaks awake and watching us.

I walk between 76 and Big as we make our way down to breakfast Saturday morning. "Don't pay any attention to those freaks in there," says 76. He's talking about the teenagers who laughed at me the day before. "They're just in a rage cuz you got to level four before they did."

Mr. Lester explained that to me before my move. Most students (prisoners) move from the first floor to the second floor and then the third floor before moving to the very top where I was going. "I'm not lookin' to give you opportunities to get into trouble, so you're not going to level two or level three," Mr. Lester had said. And for a moment I worried that I'd never leave my room. "I'm moving you to the top floor, level four. Don't make me regret it."

Mr. Lester acted like he was doing me a favor. But I know I probably hold the Great Oaks World Record for most days living on level one.

I try to pretend my ears are shut as I walk into the cafeteria. *Ignore them.* I make it through the line and sit down at the round table in the back with Big and 76. But the other teenagers are worse than school bullies. They keep pointing, laughing, and cracking jokes.

Someone calls out, "Take them off!" And soon a group starts up, "Take them off! Take them off!" At first I think they've given up on me and found someone else to pick on, until I realize they're talking about my slippers.

I walk over to the first long table and they quiet down a bit. I can see in their eyes that they're nervous, maybe even a little afraid of me. *I am a killer!*

I lift my arms and growl, "Rahhhhh!" loud and deep.

Two guys in coveralls lock my hands behind my back and pull me out of the room. "I didn't do anything! I didn't even do anything!"

I could have thrown food at them, tossed the paper plates in the air. I could have actually punched someone or broken furniture. I just uttered one word, one syllable, and I am being hauled away. Everyone else was chanting and they didn't even get into trouble. My wrists feel like they are about to snap. The guys behind me are pushing me faster than I can walk. Back in our room they march me straight to my bed and finally release me.

"Try something like that again and you'll be back on the first floor."

RIVER FALLS

Ryan still came over after school every day even though Mom wasn't home and the food wasn't as good. "We only have frozen dinners."

"It's better than my place."

Ryan walked on his hands from the front door all the way down the hall, turned around, and walked back. "I want to teach myself to climb up and down stairs on my hands," he said.

I cooked the frozen dinners in the microwave and practiced doing a handstand while they cooked. When the microwave buzzed I pulled off the plastic covers, grabbed some forks, and looked around for Ryan. "Where are you?"

"In the playroom." Ryan was sitting with his back against the wall with a line of plastic balls at his feet. He tossed a yellow one to the ball pit on the other side of the room. "Let's eat in here."

"Sitting on the floor?"

Ryan tossed another ball across the room. "Yeah, why not?"

I sat and threw a few balls. "Uncle Grant has been in the hospital forever."

Ryan rolled a ball down his arm from his shoulder to his hand.

"But your mom's been in the hospital even longer. When is she getting out?"

"How would I know?" Ryan's food was almost all gone.

"What's she in there for?"

Ryan flung a ball across the room hard. It landed in the ball pit and popped back out again. "Because I went to school, that's why."

"What?"

"I went to school and someone there complained. I got reported." He shot the balls one after another across the room. "My clothes weren't clean enough. I fell asleep. I didn't smell enough like soap."

"I don't know what you're talking about."

Ryan stood up. "You never do." He walked across the room and lay in the middle of the ball pit with his head at one end and his knees and feet sticking over the other side.

I sat against the ball pit. "So tell me. Quit leaving out half of the story."

I heard the balls sloshing while Ryan moved his arms back and forth, like a kid trying to make a snow angel. "After my dad got shot, Blast moved in with us."

"Blast?"

"That's what he was called. He was mean, a million times meaner than my dad. Just when Star was getting ready to be born he took off and we never saw him again." Ryan's arms kept swishing through the balls. "My mom cried all the time. But after Star was born, she stopped crying. She stopped doing anything; she didn't get out of bed."

Ryan's stories were always hard to believe, but this one felt as true as anything he ever told me.

"Star had to eat, that was most important. I tried to get Mom to eat, too. I tried to do everything, but...Do you know how expensive diapers are, Robbie? Do you know how hard they are to steal?"

"Robbie?" Dad called from the front door. "Come outside and see what I've got." Dad brought home a van full of wood and told us his idea. "Grant will have no trouble wheeling along the driveway to the back of the house. But that will only get him into his old apartment and the basement. We're never down there. We need a way for him to get into the rest of the house. This place needs a ramp."

He spent the weekend measuring and cutting. Ryan and I sanded and stained. Each piece of wood was soft as the shiny side of a feather after we sanded it down. But the sawdust made my skin feel like I'd spent ten years in the tub. Dad made us wear goggles, but they only helped my eyes. Every time I sniffed it felt like my nose tunnels were being sanded. I needed goggles for my nose. There was even sawdust between my teeth. I pictured the ramp finished, Dad nodding like he did when he was happy, and Uncle Grant...I couldn't picture Uncle Grant except the way he was before he left, a guy with two legs and two arms who didn't need a ramp to get into our house.

GREAT OAKS ~~SCHOOL~~ PRISON

We head to the cafeteria for lunch. Big and 76 lag behind. I try to walk between them. They walk slower and slower as we get near the door. Finally they stop and bend down.

"What is with you guys?" I ask.

They look at each other but not at me.

"You're afraid I'll get you in trouble, you'll lose tokens or something?"

Big slips something crinkly out of his pocket.

"Just go on in, Robbie," says 76.

I walk into the cafeteria. The other kids don't wait a second before they start pointing and laughing again. I'm sure they're proud of themselves for getting me into trouble. I feel their eyes on me every second. *Ignore them.* When I'm halfway to the food counter a murmer ripples through the crowd. They are looking past me at the door. The room's quiet.

Crackling feet crunch behind me—Big and 76, wearing blue plastic slippers. We get our food and sit down without saying a word, but I can't help smiling at them.

RIVER FALLS

Ryan begged me to lift the cloth and take a look at Grantville. "We've got to look at least, see if it needs cleaning."

The river was dry and dirty. Green slime covered the moat. The entire city smelled like scum. Ryan wrinkled his nose. "Told you."

I squirted some spray cleaner and wiped with paper towels.

"That won't do anything," Ryan said. He went into the laundry room and came back with a white jug.

"You think laundry soap will get this clean?" I didn't trust Ryan with Grantville.

"This is bleach. Don't you know anything?"

"Pour it on, then, cleaner guy."

"I need to mix it in a bucket with water."

Ryan bleached the moat and the river and filled them both back up with water. He poured water down the well and added blue food coloring.

I wiped off the buildings and used the mini-vac to get up all the dust. Grantville was perfect, almost. "Wait here," I said, and ran to my room. I came back and put my birthday present in the back corner, where we had planned to make the circus.

"The tigers!" Ryan leaned over and poked a finger into a tiger's mouth. "Do they jump?"

I plugged it in, counted to three, and flipped the switch.

"Awesome." Ryan's smile was huge. I knew what he was thinking: *fire*.

"Don't even think about it. We promised Uncle Grant. We didn't clean this whole thing up to have an accident and burn it down."

"I have something, too." Ryan ran upstairs and came down with a long piece of wood. The edges were jagged to make it look worn. Ryan had glued tiny pebbles onto the wood to make a sign: WELCOME TO GRANTVILLE.

I wished I had made something. Ryan's sign was perfect.

"It's great." I helped him set it up front and center.

After Ryan left, I found Dad on his computer typing away and knocked on his open door. "I have an idea for the extra wood."

GREAT OAKS ~~SCHOOL~~ PRISON

I think about my plan all weekend. I have to write a list of what I need to do to go home. I pace around the big room and try to steal glances at the TV. The guy in green coveralls finally sets up big cardboard screens making a fake wall around the TV corner of the room.

Walking circles around this room isn't helping me think. I sit on the floor and pull off my plastic slippers, shove them into my pockets. I run. I don't look out the window or try to see over the cardboard wall. I just run in big circles around the room thinking about home.

I walk one lap to cool off and stand at the window behind our beds. An army of giant oak trees stand in formation outside. They're so tall they rise above me on the fifth floor.

Big sits up on his bed and closes his book. "What's your plan, little man?"

"Still don't have one."

"Check this out." He pulls a crinkled piece of paper from his back pocket. "It's mine if it will give you any ideas."

I read Big's list. The first three lines are in perfect handwriting, like old ladies' writing:

Curtis Rodgers
1. Get my health in order—start eating again
2. Call my Grams and make sure I can move back in with her

3. Figure out how to take care of Junior—babysitting and money

Two more things are written, in Mr. Lester's scratchy printing:

4. Keep up with school work
5. Admit to the charges against me

Numbers one through four have neat little checks by them. Number five is scratched out completely. A new number five is written beneath.

5. Refrain from saying "I'm innocent" for an entire month.

There are little marks on the paper, like when you keep score by fives, four little sticks then a slanted mark through them. It looks likes Big has gone without saying "I'm innocent" for long stretches. Twelve days. Twenty-two days. Fourteen days. Eleven days. Twenty-six days.

"Firecracker! How long have you been here?"

"Forever and a week."

"Why didn't you just say you did it a long time ago and get out?"

He locks eyes with me and then glances out the window. "I'm at twenty-seven days today. I'm not about to talk on that subject."

I start to ask another question, but Big interrupts. "He made me start over again when you got to group and I said mistaken you-know-what."

"Mistaken identity?"

Big nods and makes the motion that little kids make when they are locking their lips. I hand him his paper. "Still, I would have just said, 'I did it.' Even if I didn't."

Big shrugs, clearly trying not to speak. "To each his own. But that's not my way. I started a hunger strike when I got here, trying to prove something. Maybe if you were a young black man you'd understand." He opens up his book.

"What's that got to do with it?"

Big lets out one small laugh without looking up from the page he is reading. "Are you kidding?"

"No."

Big keeps looking at his book, shakes his head, and says, "Robbie, you say some funny stuff. Make me laugh more than Junior." But he isn't laughing.

I take out a piece of paper and try to write my last list.

RIVER FALLS

Saturday, Dad and I put the sawhorses and tools in the back of the car, filled the trunk with wood and headed to Howell Street.

Ryan sat out on the porch eating bread. I wondered if it had water smeared on it.

"What the heck?" Ryan jumped up. "My grandparents aren't up yet."

"We don't need to go inside," Dad said. "I just wanted to take a look at your steps. I already spoke with your grandfather about it."

Dad measured and cut. Ryan sanded. I stained. It took half the day. At the end of it all, Ryan's grandpa came out and shook Dad's hand. Even though the old man had ten times infinity wrinkles and I could almost see through him, he wasn't as scary as before. He looked almost half human.

It took the entire week to get the ramp set up out front of our house. Dad was desperate to finish before Mom came home. He made it an important deadline, like the ones he had at work.

"I want her to be surprised," Dad said.

I knew she'd be surprised that we even started a ramp. But Dad wanted it finished and perfect. Hours before Mom came home, we attached the handrails. Dad and I stood back in the street to check it out.

The ramp was perfect.

And it wasn't perfect.

It was a ramp. For my uncle. Who couldn't walk.

Ryan came through the front door waving something orange over his head. "Watch this!"

He threw my skateboard down, jumped on, and flew down the ramp. Click-click-click the wheels ran over the joints in the wood. Ryan turned late, pivoted, and rode the final slope on two wheels. He jumped off and the skateboard skidded onto the driveway.

"Wicked!" Ryan lifted his arms and smiled.

GREAT OAKS ~~SCHOOL~~ PRISON

Mr. Lester spends the first half of group attacking 76 for not having a plan to get out of his gang. "Over the weekend you phoned three of your former friends."

76 leans forward, propping his elbows on his knees, and clenches his fists. "Just cuz I'm friends with someone don't mean I'm gonna do like they do."

Mr. Lester circles around the chairs, spitting out one word for every three steps. "You are who you associate with. If they end up in jail, you end up in jail. Step one is no contact. You have failed."

"That ain't right, man. Just a phone call is not the same as hanging with them."

Mr. Lester has made it around the circle again. He picks up his chair and lets it fall to the ground. "Contact is contact."

76 shakes his head. "I won't call them if that's what you want. I still think you're wrong. I mean, I hang with Robbie here. That don't make me a mass murderer like him."

I want to argue about the mass murderer part, but I'm too surprised that 76 sort of called me a friend.

Mr. Lester turns to me. "That's right, who do we have here? I think it's long past time we all find out more about Robbie."

RIVER FALLS

Dad and I bombarded Mom with questions about Uncle Grant. Mom tried to wear a calm face. She said, "It will be a big adjustment. His life is changed forever." A tear slid down her cheek before she could blink it back. That's all it took for two waterfalls to gush out of her eyes. She said, "It's not that bad, really. I just haven't cried yet."

Later Grandma blew into our house, tossed each of us a deck of D.C. souvenir playing cards, and said, "He's always been strong. After this he'll be stronger than ever."

I tore the plastic wrapper off my cards and thought, *He'll have to be. One side of his body will have to do double the work.*

Next to last came Grant's stuff. There was a knock on the door. Grandma opened it and didn't move or talk. The silence was like a giant hand pulling me and Mom out of the kitchen. Christy stood between two suitcases so big they made her look tiny. She looked at our door knocker and the umbrella stand, but not at us. "There are more boxes in the car."

Silence. Grandma stomped off into the kitchen. Mom and I helped Christy haul everything inside. I slid the last box up the ramp. Mom tried to invite Christy in for dinner, for coffee, for cake. She offered Christy every kind of food we had in the house.

Mom made one last try. "Let's just talk."

Christy shook her head. "I'm going. If Grant wants anything else..." She finally looked down at me. "Bye, Robbie."

Grandma had only two words to say when the door closed. "Good riddance."

I'm not stupid. I guessed Grant and Christy were breaking up again.

"He can stay here again, for a while," said Mom.

GREAT OAKS ~~SCHOOL~~ PRISON

Mr. Lester motions for me to stand up. "Are you a mass murderer, Robbie?"

I stand and face him. "No."

"Who are you?"

"No one."

Mr. Lester bends over me; he's close to my face. "Who are you?" I back away. With each step I take back, he moves closer. I feel the wall at my back. "Answer me!"

"Just Robbie."

He grabs my arms, pins them to my sides, and lifts me. "Are you a killer?"

My feet are off the ground. I kick the air, arch my back, try to kick him. "Yes!" I scream as loudly as I can, wanting to break his ears.

"A murderer?"

I can't move my arms, can't fight back. "Yes! Let me go! Put me down!"

"Do you go around beating kids for fun?"

"Put me down." I lean side to side, but he just grabs me tighter. I try to reach him with my head, bash him in the nose.

"Do you even remember who you were before you killed Ryan?"

"Let go!" I cry.

76 is half standing, frozen in place.

"Who is Robbie?" asks Mr. Lester.

"No one!" I scream.

"Tell me!" Mr. Lester's breath blows my hair. His fingers crush my arms.

"I—"

Big meets my eyes. "Tell him, Robbie. Triple T."

"I didn't want to do it! I didn't even try to do it!" I let my body go limp, praying I will slide though his arms.

Mr. Lester lets me sag onto the floor. "That's what I thought. Triple T, Robbie. Tell us about Ryan."

Big, 76, and Mr. Lester watch me climb into my seat. I rub my arms where Mr. Lester held me, tortured me. Why is it that when something terrible happens, people just try to forget it as soon as possible? I should call 'triple T' on Mr. Lester. *Tell us, why do you like to pick on kids?* But instead, I try to find the right words to describe Ryan.

"Ryan smelled like lemons. I didn't know why for the longest time, until I caught him in the kitchen smearing dish soap up the insides of his arms. He even put some at the back of his neck. He did all kinds of strange things like that.

"He was just a kid, a new kid at school, and he started hanging around our house. For the food, at first. And because my mom is nice to everyone. He loved Mom's daycare, especially the babies. I didn't like him at first, but..."

Mr. Lester doesn't interrupt. 76 and Big barely move. They don't try to get me to hurry up and talk. It is like those staring contests you have when you're a kid. *How long will they stay quiet if I just sit here?*

I stand up and walk around the circle, like Mr. Lester does when he's really mad. It is easier to talk and walk. It is easier to think without three pairs of eyes staring at me.

"I could never believe what Ryan said because he said so many strange things. Like that his dad was a drug dealer who got shot and his Mom didn't get out of bed after she had a baby. Ryan had to take care of his little sister all by himself. He used to collect cans to get money to buy food. He said he stole diapers for the baby. I mean, nothing he said was normal."

Big nods like my talking about Ryan reminds him of someone he knows. 76 is still looking at the floor.

"Sometimes he'd get courageous. He fought a big bully to save a baby kitten. He broke into the construction lot, not to steal anything, just to play." I stop walking and stand behind my seat. "Ryan loved to play with little kids. He would tell them jokes, paint, he'd do anything for them. He even walked on his hands..."

I plop into my chair feeling like I forgot to say something, something important, about Ryan. "He got a bunch of kids from school to come to my races and cheer me for me at the finish line."

I wait for Mr. Lester to attack his next victim. "Sounds like he was your friend," he says.

RIVER FALLS

I stood at the top of the ramp by the front door. Dad lugged a wheelchair out of the trunk while Mom opened Uncle Grant's door. Before he could get out, Grandma dived in and hugged him. Uncle Grant used the roof of the car to pull himself up. He turned and fell into the wheelchair.

I stayed where I was, stuck. I wanted to run to the car and see him, but part of me wanted to back all the way into the house. Dad pushed the wheelchair.

"There's my man," said Uncle Grant. He lifted his arm for a high five.

I hit his hand, but not too hard.

"That's all you got? Don't need to go easy on me just because I'm a cripple."

I looked away.

"Hey, I'm just joking. Besides, I've been lifting weights. Twice a day."

He lifted his arm up again and I hit it harder. Not real hard, just harder.

Dad pushed Uncle Grant into the living room and we all sat down and stared for a second. I tried not to look at his arm and leg, his missing arm and leg. But my eyes kept going back, like a tongue pushing on a sore spot even though it hurts.

"Scoot over, Mom. I don't want to stay in this chair." Grandma scooted and Uncle Grant plopped onto the sofa beside her. "Dang,

Robbie! You've grown a foot! Get over here and let me see you."

I sat down next to him. Uncle Grant smelled like medicine and sweat. Not exercise sweat like after a run. He stank of old-people sweat, sweet and dusty-smelling, like Grandma's friends sitting around playing cards.

We learned in school that a dog can tell the difference between people by the smell of their sweat. One single dog could tell 218,000 people apart just from their smell. But would a dog notice if the same person had a new kind of sweat?

I could.

Two people had no problem talking to Uncle Grant about his injuries. One was Ryan. The other was his physical therapist.

Ryan asked a trillion questions about camping out, fighting the enemy, and every single detail of the war. Ryan said stupid stuff. The first time he saw Uncle Grant he blurted, "So what happened? How'd you get injured?"

Uncle Grant said, "Let's just talk about something else for today, buddy."

I thought he'd change the subject. Instead Ryan said, "I saw on TV about this guy got his leg blown off like you and he was going back. Got a fake leg and went right back to the battlefield. You going back?"

"Shut up," I said.

But Uncle Grant answered him. "No. I don't plan to. It's not something I want to go through again."

Ryan started to open his mouth, but I stopped him. "Shut up, already!"

"I was just going to tell him about what we did."

Uncle Grant had to wheel outside, down the ramp, around the house and in the back door to get to his apartment in the basement. Robbie and I lifted up the cover to Grantville.

"Hey, it looks great. Better than I remembered it. That sign is totally medieval."

The physical therapist was a tall, skinny lady named Glenda. She came to our house. Glenda called Uncle Grant's injured arm and leg "stumps." She tugged elastic wrap around his leg until he told her, "That's tight enough. I can't take any more." She made him do exercises. Anytime anyone laughed, she laughed louder.

Glenda saw me watching one day and waved me over. "This your brother?"

I shook my head. "My uncle."

"Well, your uncle here is a big fat cheater." Uncle Grant just laughed. Glenda laughed louder. She dug into the pocket of her white coat and pulled out a thick red marker. "Now, we're gonna get this stump facing straight." She looked at me and winked. "Without a foot pointing the way it's kinda hard to tell." She put a hand on Uncle Grant's hip and told him to turn his leg. "It's rolled out to the side. Roll it in. More. More. Even more."

When Uncle Grant's leg was finally in the right position, she drew a long line down the front. Not just on the bandage, she drew on his skin. Then she put two little lines on the top. "That's an 'F' for 'front.' See that?"

I nodded.

"Good, because you're my assistant. And your uncle here's gotta do these exercises when I'm not here. You need to watch and make sure the F is pointing up at the ceiling. Otherwise he has to start over. Got it?"

"Yeah," I said.

She laughed so loud it hurt my ears. Uncle Grant just smiled. "Robbie, you know what 'P.T.' stands for?"

"Physical therapy," I said.

"Pain and torture," he answered.

They both cracked up.

GREAT OAKS ~~SCHOOL~~ PRISON

Mr. Lester stops me at the circle desk before I can slip back into the room. He passes my list back. I had written only one thing:

Robbie Thompson
1. Pass seventh grade

"Do you really think you're here to do schoolwork, Robbie?" he asks.

"You guys are the ones who call it Great Oaks School."

Mr. Lester had added two more items to the list.

2. Talk about Ryan in group
3. Apologize

I've already started number two today, but number three? Impossible.

"Sign the bottom to show you agree." Mr. Lester holds out a pen. When I don't reach for the pen he says, "Hurry up. I have something else for you."

Great. I sign the paper even though I don't know if I can keep doing number two or ever accomplish number three.

Mr. Lester smiles and hands me a pair of old running shoes.

"My shoes! My shoes!"

"Put them on and follow me. You have a visitor."

RIVER FALLS

One day when Ryan was over talking war talk, Uncle Grant sent me downstairs. "Look in the top drawer of my dresser on the left side. There's a box. Don't open it. Bring it here so I can show you both." I brought it to him.

Uncle Grant turned the small box in his hand. He rubbed his thumb across the front of it. "Have any idea what this is?" Uncle Grant flipped his thumb up and the top of the box lifted.

Inside was a pendant on the end of a purple ribbon. It was a circle and a heart and the gold head of a man.

"Purple Heart," said Ryan like a person on a game show.

As soon as he said it, I knew he was right. I wished I had said it first.

Ryan oohed and aahed. "It's your Purple Heart. You earned a Purple Heart."

Uncle Grant sort of laughed. "It's not something you try to earn. But yeah. It's mine. I was awarded it."

At school, I read an article about Uncle Grant for News of the Day. I brought the news clipping with me to the front of the class even though I had it memorized. I read, "On this date outside the city of Tikrit, Iraq, two U.S. servicemen were killed and three injured by an improvised explosive device. Names withheld pending notification of family members."

No one in the class said anything. They heard the same thing or something like it every day on the news. "I was one of the family members. This is the article about when my uncle was hurt."

Mr. Michaels stood up. "RST, see me after school."

After school Mr. Michaels pointed to my news article displayed with the others. "Yours. Get it down." I did what he said. "Now, Robbie, I didn't want to embarrass you in front of the class..."

Really? That was a first.

"You will not bring any more such articles to class. Do you remember what I said about the war?" I shook my head. Mr. Michaels never talked about the war. It was like it didn't exist. "I told you that you can come after school and talk to me anytime, but not to mention the war in my classroom."

But what about news of the day? Wasn't the war news of the day? I didn't say anything.

"Write 'I will listen to my teacher' 500 times for tomorrow morning."

I just stared at him. I didn't do anything wrong. I read a news article. It is what we were supposed to do. I was so sick of getting in trouble for no reason.

"I'll be here awhile if you want to stay and write now." Mr. Michaels smiled like he was offering me something good, like a piece of cake.

"I'll write it at home," I told him.

But I didn't. Instead of sitting down and writing "I will listen to my teacher," I went out and killed somebody.

GREAT OAKS ~~SCHOOL~~ PRISON

My shoes squish my feet, but I walk as fast as I can. A visitor. I hope this is for real. *What if he's moving me back to level one? What if it he's taped me talking in group and the police are here to talk about Ryan?* We walk all the way down to the first floor.

Mr. Lester stops in front of a wooden door with a golden doorknob. "I'm giving you this opportunity only because I think you're ready. Don't screw it up."

He opens the door to a room with big windows and chairs lined up around the walls, a waiting room. Uncle Grant sits flipping through a magazine. I barely notice the door closing behind me as Mr. Lester steps out of the room.

"Uncle Grant!"

Uncle Grant stands up. His prosthetic leg is off, standing in front of his chair. He hops over and hugs me tight. "My man. My man!"

"What are you doing here? Is everything okay?"

Uncle Grant sits and rubs the end of his short leg, his stump. "I'm here to make sure you're okay."

Finally! "Mom and Dad, are they here, too?" I walk across the room. Heavy curtains cover the windows; the only door leads to the hallway.

"They wanted to, but they couldn't get permission from this place. Your dad's actually out in the car. That Lester guy said you could have a visitor as long as it wasn't your mom or dad. So, what's the story? You okay?"

I plop down next to him. *Am I okay?* I can't even think of words to answer that question. Back when I was stuck alone in my room, this was my favorite daydream. Mom or Dad would show up, I'd tell them how horrible it was here, and we'd dash out the door to freedom and never look back.

"Robbie?" Uncle Grant's voice is high-pitched and singsong, the way he used to say my name when he was trying to wake me up.

"I'm mostly okay. I guess. I just want to get out of here as soon as possible." I want to let it all rush out. No privileges. Being locked up on the first floor. Mr. Lester. But Mr. Lester's warning catches me before I start talking. *I think you're ready. Don't screw it up.*

I lose my voice. Great Oaks is impossible to explain to someone who hasn't lived here. "I have some things I have to do first. My studies. And other stuff. But I think I'm close to getting out. Closer than I've ever been."

Uncle Grant pulls his pant leg up and rubs his stump again. It's all healed, no more bandages. He runs his fingernails across the end of his leg real fast, like he's scratching a dog behind the ears. "Forgot my medicine. Feels like I got a foot sometimes. Crud between my toes and everything. Totally weird." He looks me up and down. "You're skinny, even for you. Do they feed you enough around here? Are you working out?"

I wiggle in my chair. "I'm eating enough now. I exercise some."

"I'm back to running. Made the cut for the Warrior Games. Running the 1,500-meter race."

"How can you even... I mean, does it hurt?"

"Hurt at first. Hurt my wallet, too, getting the right equipment." Uncle Grant laughs. "It's worth every penny, though, just to be able to run again."

I can't tell Grant about my running—alone in my room on the first floor or pathetic little laps around the fifth-floor living area.

"Robbie, come on, more about you. I'll hear about it from your parents and my ma if I just sit here and talk about myself all day. I got a long ride home with your dad."

Dad is sitting out in the parking lot. I walk to the window and pull open the curtains, but I don't see Dad's car.

"Where's Dad?"

"We're parked on the other side, by the front entrance."

I want to punch the window, shatter the glass and run to my dad. He drove all the way here and we can't see each other.

"I'd give you my cell phone to call him," says Uncle Grant. "Heck, I'd let you keep it so you can call us whenever you want. But they made me empty my pockets before meeting you."

I sit next to Uncle Grant. "Tell Dad I wish I could see him. And Mom." I feel like everything in the world is my fault.

"Hey, we're all rooting for you. We know you're going through something terrible. No kid, no person, should have to deal with this."

I can barely hear him. "I'm sorry for Ryan. Sorry I got stuck in this firecracker school away from everyone."

Uncle Grant says, "Firecracker?"

I kinda laugh. "It's a word we use to swear."

Uncle Grant looks at me to see if I'm serious. "Okay. Understood."

I try to blink back tears. My nose starts running and the room is getting blurry. Finally someone is here. Someone who really cares about what happens to me.

Uncle Grant lifts his left arm, the one with the fake hand, to reach for me, and stops in midair. He pats the seat on the other side of him. "Sit over here, will you?"

I move over and he reaches out to hold me. "Cry if you need to. It helps. I know that for a fact."

I barely hear him. Everything is my fault. And there is nothing I can do about it. "I'm sorry about your leg and arm."

Uncle Grant gives a chuckle. "Me too, my man, me too."

I sit up and brush my cheeks. "No, I mean I'm *sorry*. It's all my fault."

Uncle Grant shakes his head. "Robbie, my injuries? None of that is your fault."

I take a breath. I take three breaths so deep and long that I feel a little dizzy, like when I swim to the bottom of the pool to get a stone and have to fight my way up against all the water just to breathe. "Before you left, you told me. You said you were going over there, to the war, for me. If it weren't for me..." I feel like I'm falling underwater again.

"No way. I went there because it was my job. I wanted to go." He runs his hand through his hair. "I feel the same as you. If I hadn't shown you two kids that Purple Heart..."

I fall back against his chest. It's easier to talk when we aren't looking at each other. My tears are gone. I stare at the dust floating in the room. The sun rays sneak through the space where the curtains join and make the dust look like rainbow sparkles. It isn't Uncle Grant's fault—me and Ryan's big fight, our last fight.

"I got in trouble for reading a news article about you to the class."

Seventh grade seems like a hundred years ago. Mr. Michaels used to scare me. "I read the *Stars and Stripes* article about the explosion, about when you were hurt. My teacher wouldn't let us talk about the war. I had to stay after school. When I caught up with...with *Ryan*, he had snuck into the construction site."

I see everything like it is happening again, like watching a movie. Uncle Grant's chest is moving slow and even, like someone asleep. But I know he isn't.

"Ryan was sitting at the edge of that big hole, holding your Purple Heart. I told him to give it to me. He snapped the box shut and tossed it to me. When he ran away, I knew he still had the Purple Heart. I flipped the box open and it was empty."

THE FIGHT

I sprinted after Ryan, the velvet box sweaty in my hand. He dodged between the machines, slowed down to run around the corner of the enormous hole. I jumped at him and caught one of his feet. The instant he hit the ground, I lunged forward and sat on his legs.

"Give it back," I said.

"Owwww—" Ryan tried to kick me off.

I pushed both of my arms on his back, planting him. "Give it, Ryan."

Ryan twisted and turned over. But he couldn't shake me off. His face was streaked with dirt. He held up both his hands. Empty.

"Now you see it. Now you don't." He smirked.

He rocked side to side, took a swipe at my chest and missed. Ryan balled up both of his fists and attacked my legs. I socked him hard in the gut.

"Give it now!" I locked my elbows and pushed down on his shoulders.

He punched my arm. "I hate you," he spat.

"I hate you, too!"

At that moment, I did hate Ryan. I hated him for coming to our town, my school. I hated him for eating at our house, for pretending to be my friend. I even hated him for living in a falling-down house without enough to eat.

Ryan pushed both my arms aside and started punching me like a maniac. I rolled over, out of the way, and he was on top of me in a second. His fist connected under my jaw, his open palm slapped my cheek—hard. I turned my head and saw his fist flying right at my face. My nose exploded. Fireworks splashed in my head, sticky heat oozed down my face and into my mouth. Blood.

Ryan slid off of me and sat in the dirt. "Poor Robbie."

I wiped my eyes, smearing blood across my face. I wasn't thinking about the medal. I wanted him to hurt. I wanted to strike blood.

Ryan stared at me. His arms were wrapped around his knees and his face was blank.

I stood up, waiting for him to say something, do something. My lower lip swelled. My tongue pressed against each of my teeth to be sure none were loose, or missing.

Ryan ignored me. He stretched out his legs, leaned back on his arms, and brought one hand forward, pretending to yawn.

My face was covered in blood.

And he pretended to be bored.

I jumped on top of him, landing hard. My fists flew into his chest, his face. Ryan lifted his arms in front of his face and I pounded them, too.

"Stop! Stop!" he hollered.

I kept hitting until he was quiet.

"Give—it—back!" I growled, landing a punch in his side with every word.

Ryan's arms were still in front of his face. "You have so many medals, Robbie. For all of your stupid races. I have nothing. Nothing!"

"It's not yours. It's not even mine, you freak!" I put a hand on the ground and leaned over to get up.

Ryan rolled on top of me. He sat on my hips and started

punching my chest. "Take that!" Punch. "And that!" Punch. Ryan's mouth and fists worked together. He had to say something with every punch. Each punch struck harder, deeper, as though Ryan was actually getting stronger the more he hit me. He pounded my ear and I felt heat pierce my skull and heard a high, buzzing noise.

His thuds softened. For a moment I thought he was winding down. My stomach jerked like I was waking up from a falling dream, and I felt the full force of his fists again.

He hadn't slowed down. I was fading away.

My blood was everywhere, my nose, my lips, my ear. It dripped on my face and seeped into my skin. I could taste it. I swung, but my hands didn't connect.

"I hate you," I croaked out.

"I," punch. "Hate," punch. "You," punch. "Too," punch. I tried to grab Ryan's arms, but they were moving too fast.

I swallowed; blood coated my throat. Ryan was going to keep punching until there was nothing left of me. Panic bubbled up from my stomach. I knew the only way I could survive was to get away.

"Ahhhh!" I screamed. "I'm going to kill you!" I bent my knees and bucked my hips. I grabbed his shoulders and yanked him forward, crashing his head against my bloody nose. I shoved him to the side, pushed him as hard as I could until he rolled away.

I got to my knees. I wanted to run before he could catch me again, but my head was swimming. It took a long time to stand up. I turned in a circle, searching, but Ryan was gone.

A splash of blue and green lay sprawled on the dirt at the bottom of the enormous hole.

Blue jeans.

Green shirt.

Ryan.

I'd never seen him so still.

The purple box lay open in the dirt, tossed aside during the fight. I reached for it, the velvet soft against my grimy hands. I snapped the empty box closed.

Ryan was dead.

And I was a murderer.

GREAT OAKS ~~SCHOOL~~ PRISON

The room seems to move up and down with Uncle Grant's breathing. It hurts down inside my chest to talk about the fight, like I am pulling out broken pieces of glass that are deep under my skin.

"I told him I would do it, Uncle Grant. I told him, 'I'm going to kill you.' And I hated him more than anything." I can't blink back tears anymore. Ryan's voice rings in my ears and so do my own words, threatening to kill him.

"I told the police it was an accident. But when I remember it, I hear my voice, those words. It makes me think..."

I swallow and admit the truth. "It makes me think that I really wanted to." Uncle Grant tightens his arm around me. He doesn't say anything. "I have nightmares. I hear myself say it. The worst thing is that right then, I wanted him dead."

Uncle Grant clears his throat. "Robbie..."

"I told everyone that it was an accident. That he rolled. He fell. But I did it. I was the one who pushed him. I wanted to kill him when he was hitting me. I was so angry, not just about the Purple Heart, about everything."

Uncle Grant squeezes me tight.

I whisper, "Sometimes I still hate him. I'm so mad."

"I know," says Uncle Grant.

I close my eyes. "I didn't *try* to kill him. I didn't know we were that close to the edge." I block out everything and drift off until I'm halfway asleep. I'm not thinking about Ryan or Mr. Lester or even

Uncle Grant. With my eyes closed, I imagine the room around us with rainbow dust swirling in the air.

Uncle Grant's voice seems to come from far away, like when a DVD is playing but the TV isn't switched over so you hear the movie words with the TV picture. "I was in the wrong place at the right time," Uncle Grant says. His breathing lifts my head up and down.

"One of my buddies, Sergeant Davis, we switched places." He stops for a second and catches his breath. "I won't go into everything, but we switched places and later he jogged up to me and said he was feeling better, he wanted to move up front."

I don't understand what Uncle Grant is saying.

"We knew every day we'd find the IEDs, the hidden bombs. It was our job to look for them. Sergeant Davis wasn't feeling well. I told him I could handle it up front."

Uncle Grant moves his arm away and I sit up. The room isn't all sparkly like I had imagined. Instead it looks worn and gray. "I haven't told anyone this, Robbie. Sergeant Davis and another buddy of mine died that day and I lived. If I had changed places with him, if I had done what he asked, he'd be alive."

I'm glad that Uncle Grant is the one alive.

But I know how he feels.

GREAT OAKS ~~SCHOOL~~ PRISON

Mr. Lester is waiting for me outside the door after my visit with Uncle Grant. *Did he hear everything?* "I'll take your shoes," he says.

I take them off, dig my slippers out of my pocket, and head up to the fifth floor.

I can't sleep at night. Big is awake, too, pacing and looking out the window; he's going home in the morning. He notices me with my eyes open, glued to the ceiling. I feel the air move as he walks back and forth. But we don't talk.

In the morning, Big promises to call and keep in touch. 76 says, "Don't believe him, Robbie. Big and I seen a buncha fellas come and go enough to know that's a flat-out lie. Every single one of those firecrackers talk about callin'. Don't blame them, though." 76 sighs. "Once I'm home free I won't give this place or you peeps one single thought."

Big asks Mr. Lester to let me and 76 meet his grandma and his kid. Junior gives Big this drooly smile and starts to giggle. He half runs, half waddles over to Big. And as much as Big talks about Junior all the time, I never really thought of him as a dad until I see them together. It's weird. Big is a dad. He is a teenager and a dad.

Still, the baby is just a regular goo-goo, gah-gah drooling baby trying to run. He isn't the super genius kid that Big makes him out to be. Big's grandma holds her arms out and takes the baby. Big shakes Mr. Lester's hand, gives me a pat on the back and actually hugs 76. He picks up his suitcase and strolls down the walk to his grandma's car.

We're all quiet marching up the stairs to the fifth floor. 76 says, "Cheer up, Robbie. You get your first tokens today. I say we celebrate and I whip your ass in Ping-Pong."

"Nope. I want to use my tokens to call home."

HOME

Mr. Lester lectures me for an hour before my visit home. "Most kids start by going out to lunch or maybe home for a few hours. They build up to overnight. I've never ever sent someone home for a whole weekend right off the bat. Never."

I've passed every test for seventh grade. English. History. Math. Science. World Cultures. It's not like it was hard or anything. Anyone who can read the chapters and answer the questions in the back of the book can pass the stupid tests. There really isn't a school at Great Oaks.

Mom and Dad want me home for a whole weekend. Mom can't make the long drive here, and staying home for only a few hours is just stupid. "We need time to get comfortable together again," Mom said on the phone last night. Whatever that means.

When Mr. Lester and I make it downstairs, Dad's standing in the lobby. He reaches over and hugs me without saying a word. We walk to the car together as if we haven't spent months and months apart. Everything outside looks bigger and cleaner than I remember. Even the stop signs and streetlights look bright and new.

It starts sprinkling on the way home. As Dad waits for the guard at Sunny Springs to lift the gate, it begins to pour. The house, our house, is wet and blurry through the windshield. I step into the rain and lift my face to the sky. My shirt sticks to me and I imagine I'm standing under a waterfall.

The water stops instantly. I open my eyes and Dad is smiling in front of me under a big golf umbrella. "I have your backpack," he says.

I walk up the ramp. Dad puts a hand on my wet shoulder. "No one uses the stairs anymore. The daycare parents loved it. The playroom was like stroller city."

The daycare is closed now. I squish up the stairs and find Mom in bed. She looks like she hasn't slept in days, but her face zaps to life when she sees me. She doesn't care that I'm dripping wet. I sit on the edge of her bed and lean forward for a hug. She grabs me like she'll never let go. She says, "Finally, you're home. Finally." Over and over again.

When she lets go her cheek is wet from my hair. I say, "Finally, I can take a breath. Finally." The words are true. I am breathing differently at home.

"I wish I weren't stuck in bed." Mom smiles and pushes her hair behind her ears. She rubs her stomach. "Not much longer, though."

I check out her belly. It looks like she stuck a beach ball under her shirt.

"Do you feel sick?"

"I feel great. That's the problem. I have so much energy. I keep thinking of everything I have to do. Everything I want to do."

Dad pokes his head into the bedroom. "I gotta take him. The school won't be open tomorrow." Dad and I have an appointment to register for school. He looks me over and sets my backpack in the hallway. "And you need to change your shirt."

Mom squeezes my hand like I'm going away for a long time again.

"Ouch." I jerk my hand away and rub it.

"Sorry. Don't know my own strength," she says. I bend over and kiss her cheek.

I don't want to rush out now that I'm finally here. I want to see if my room is the same. I want to see what projects are down in the basement, explore the attic. I want to search every corner of this house and make myself belong here again.

I tug a red shirt out of my backpack and walk to the laundry room. As I toss my wet shirt into the hamper by the washing machine, Dad honks. I hurry without stopping to put my shirt on.

At the bottom of the stairs I don't head straight to the front door, but turn. The fridge glimmers in the kitchen. One huge enormous giant refrigerator full of food. Food I haven't had in months, like soda and junk food, food with actual real sugar in it. I turn the corner. A thin girl with short, dark hair stands at our kitchen counter folding laundry. Her back is to me.

Chocolate milk. Pudding cups. Pepsi.

The girl stretches out a blue-and-white bath towel before folding it.

Ice pops. Ice cream sandwiches. Candy bars.

Go get food, it's just a girl.

Dad honks again. I step into the kitchen. The girl turns. "Robbie?"

Anna Beth Carter.

"What happened to your hair?" I ask, and realize I'm holding my shirt, not wearing it.

Her hands fly to her neck. "Do you think it's too short? Does it look okay?"

"Um. It's okay." What do I know about girl hair? I slip my shirt over my head.

"Yours is longer than mine now." She's right. I've been pushing my bangs out of my eyes for a few weeks. She glances over at the laundry. "I just help your mom with stuff."

Dad beeps, long and impatient this time. "Okay," I say, and hurry out the door. When I buckle my seat belt I realize I didn't grab any food.

A thick folder of papers from the six schools I attended in the past year sits on the seat beside me. I flip through it. There's a three-page progress report from Mr. Lester. It lists all the subjects

I'd studied, my grades, and test scores. The final section is my favorite: "Robert has completed all required coursework for the seventh grade. I recommend that he enter eighth grade."

The lady in the office has short, black hair and a face full of piercings. Her computer hums like an old car. She shakes Dad's hand and pulls out a file of papers. Then she starts bossing Dad around. "Shot records?" He hands them over.

"Last report card?" He gives her the whole folder.

She types on the computer and scribbles with a pen. *Tap tap tap, scribble scribble scribble. Tap tap tap.* I count the rings on her face. Three silver rings in her left eyebrow, five in the right. One ring in her upper lip and a tiny diamond in her nose. She looks up, sees me staring at her, and smiles. She's pretty. I never thought a grown-up could be pretty like that. Her dark hair, pale skin, and silvery face fit just right with her smile.

Mom apologizes all weekend because Uncle Grant and Grandma are out of town at a poker tournament. "They were on the road before we got permission for your visit. Once he told us you could come, we didn't want to wait. I wish we could have planned a party for you."

Nothing I say convinces her that just being home is enough. I don't want a party.

"Grandma's on a winning streak," Mom tells me. "You know her, trying to win big."

I don't explore the attic, but search every inch of my room. My closet holds clothes that are too small for me. I avoid two places—the basement, because it doesn't feel right to go down there without Uncle Grant, and the Internet, because I don't even know anyone to game with or chat with anymore.

Mom lets me bake a batch of homemade cookies all by myself. I walk up the stairs to ask her what to do next and then walk down to the kitchen. I pull the first batch of cookies out of the oven and eat one right off the cookie sheet while it is still burning hot. It is melty and falling apart and it is the best cookie I've ever tasted in my life.

Mom climbs down the stairs Sunday night and we swing on the porch. She is quieter than ever, but she seems happier than ever, too.

"We're going to name the baby Regina, after your grandmother."

The baby is a girl? I've been expecting a little brother.

Mom pushes the swing back with the tips of her toes. "Uncle Grant was about the age you are now when you were born." I know this already. "We let him pick out your middle name." I know this, too, but for some reason parents like talking about things that happened before you can remember, so I let Mom go on and on. "Your dad wanted your middle name to be Alexander, but Grant said Sander was a cooler name and it would be good luck because of Winnie-the-Pooh."

I smile and finish the story for her. "Because Pooh lived in a tree under the name of Sanders." Uncle Grant used to read me stories about Pooh when I was little, but I don't remember Pooh being very lucky in any of them.

"We haven't come up with a middle name for Regina yet. But there's still time." Mom rubs her belly in little circles.

GREAT OAKS ~~SCHOOL~~ PRISON

"Welcome home, Robbie." Mr. Lester stands at the front of Great Oaks as if he knew the exact moment Dad would be dropping me off.

"This is not my home. I don't see why I have to stay here another week anyway. Everything is fine at home."

Mr. Lester props the door open with his hip. "Fine today's not the same as fine tomorrow."

He points me into the group room without even giving me a chance to take my bag to my room. "Now we start what I call 'transition work.' We plan for the likely and the unlikely."

He grabs a chair and turns it backward before sitting down, leaning his chin on the back of the chair. "It's likely the kids at school are going to remember what happened with Ryan and they'll ask you about it. What are you going to tell them?"

I shrug. "It depends."

"That is not a specific enough answer. What are you going to say?"

"I don't know." It's the truth, triple T, quadruple T, infinity T, the total truth.

"Well, now's the time to find out. Stand up, right there in the middle of the room." I move to where he's pointing and watch while he pushes the other chairs to the side of the room. "You're at school and I'm another student, got it?"

"Um...okay."

Mr. Lester starts at the far corner of the room and walks in my direction; he starts to walk past me but stops all of a sudden. "Hey, I know you. Robbie, right?"

"Yes," I say. It will be good to see some of my old friends again. Some of them will remember me, I bet.

"You're the one who killed that other kid, aren't you?"

"Um..." I try to think of a way to change the subject.

Mr. Lester steps to the side, pretends to be someone else. "What did you say? He's the kid who killed that boy last year?" Mr. Lester keeps moving to the side, acting like more and more people and filling the air with words about me being a killer.

I feel like a crowd is pushing in on me, and take a few steps back. *This is just Mr. Lester, only one person, and we're not at school.*

I keep taking steps back until I'm up against the wall. "What's the matter? Are you afraid of me?" Mr. Lester is right up in my face.

"I'm not afraid of anything," I say, and we both know it is a lie.

Mr. Lester backs up to one of the chairs and motions for me to sit next to him. It takes me a moment to realize that he's back to being Mr. Lester and not pretending to be a kid anymore. When I sit down he gives a long sigh. "You must remember what you've learned here," he says.

But it doesn't seem like I've learned anything. I've just been trapped, waiting to get out.

Mr. Lester says, "It all goes back to that first list. It's all about who you are."

Earl shows up with two lunch trays. Mr. Lester must have planned this, to keep me in here with him all day.

Meatloaf, creamed corn, spinach, and a brown-and-white salad. *How could I have ever thought Great Oaks' food was good?* "What kind of salad is this?" I ask Mr. Lester.

He scoops a forkful and tastes it. "Mushroom and onion.

Now, we need to talk about your strategies when you go back to school."

Mr. Lester lectures and lectures and lectures. He could have written his advice down in a neat little list.

Reactions when people ask about Ryan

1. Be direct and honest: Yes that was me and I don't want to talk about it.
2. Be honest and change the subject
3. Change the subject without answering the question
4. Be confrontational (verbally)
5. Be aggressive (physically)

Of course, only one through three are acceptable to Mr. Lester. We act for another couple of hours. Finally I tell him, "I'm ready now. I get it."

Mr. Lester laughs. "We're done for now, but you're not ready for anything. I went easy on you today. This is just day one."

On Tuesday, Mr. Lester finds me at breakfast and tells me to meet him again. I stop in my room for a new pair of plastic slippers. They crinkle as I walk the long hallway.

Mr. Lester is standing in the group room waiting for me, his arms crossed over his chest. "It could be that some boys in your class, or older kids, tough girls even, may want to prove how tough they are by taking you on. Think you're ready for that?"

Part of me thinks that if I can survive Great Oaks, I can survive anything. Another part of me remembers how much I hate fights. I hate being without friends. I even hate eating in the cafeteria without 76.

Mr. Lester doesn't give me a second to get ready. He starts right in, "There's Robbie. Robbie the weirdo." I look down at my feet. None of the strategies from yesterday will work here. "You are a freaky little kid. Where did you go? Did they lock you up? Why aren't you locked up?"

I can't help it, I back up again. One small step at a time until my back is against the wall. Ugly words, disgusting words, explode like vomit from his mouth.

"You should be in jail, psycho boy!" He hollers right in my face. "Psycho freakoid. Freaktopia." I clench my fists. It takes more strength not to fight than it would to swing at him right now. The names accumulate in my mind: psycho, weirdo, loser.

"You are a freak, Robbie." Mr. Lester's voice sounds like a memory. The fighting voices. Ryan, even. It happens in a split second. Suddenly the man in front of me isn't really Mr. Lester. He's everything I hate. He's Ryan. He's the fight. He's my past. Every horrible thing I hate about myself is right in front of me calling me names.

I can't ignore him. I pull back my fist and let it fly at the wall. And another punch. And another. The skin peels away from my knuckles like a skinned knee.

Mr. Lester keeps talking. "Don't you want to hit me? Come on, punch me. I know it's not that wall you're mad at. Lay one on me."

I want to, but if I hit him, if I even take a swing at him and miss, I won't get home. "Stop!" I yell back. "Why are you still doing this? Just stop!"

I kick the wall hard, again and again, until my big toe is numb.

"You're a real tough kid, aren't you? Attacking a wall? Come on, it's me you want to fight. Fight me!"

I fall to the floor, hug my knees and lean my head forward. When he finally stops, the room vibrates with quiet.

I look up and ask, "Did I pass?"

"What do you think?" He isn't loud now, but his voice is rough.

"I didn't hit you. I passed."

Mr. Lester shakes his head. His face is bright pink. "We'll have at it again tomorrow. It's good you didn't hit me. But we're aiming for you not getting angry at all."

Back in the room, I lie in bed sucking the scrapes on my hand. Tomorrow a grown man is going to scream in my face, call me names, and try to get me to punch him.

I am not supposed to get angry at all.

I remember the riddle Grandma sent me. I will have to do the impossible. I try to think of a plan, but I fall asleep before dinner and sleep through the night.

GREAT OAKS ~~SCHOOL~~ PRISON

The alarm clock buzzes long and loud at six A.M. I am starving. I dress and shake 76 awake.

"I'm starving," I say. "I'm going to eat."

"Right behind you."

I head down to the cafeteria. Back when I was on the first floor, it was the highlight of the day whenever anyone came into my room, especially someone with food. Earl helped me out on my first day. He wasn't supposed to talk to me, but he did. One person breaking the rules a little made me feel like a human instead of a prisoner.

I never thanked him for bringing me breakfast every day. I guess I didn't want to seem stupid. He was just doing his job.

76 brings his tray over to my table. He must have a test today, because he brought a history book with him.

I gobble down my breakfast and try to come up with something to use against Mr. Lester. I know what he will say. I know what he will do.

"Firecracker!" I drop my fork. It is all I can do to keep eating. I want to run to the group room. I can't wait to get started.

"What?" 76 looks around the cafeteria.

"Nothing," I say. But it is something. I have a whole new way of looking at everything. Mr. Lester is just doing his job. I close my eyes and imagine our next session.

In the group room, Mr. Lester rubs his hands together before we start. "You ready?" he asks. I nod, force myself not to smile, and try to keep a poker face.

In the blink of an eye Mr. Lester changes character, pretends he is one of my future classmates. "So you the big, tough killer boy?" He does an excellent impersonation of a kid.

"Yes," I say.

"I'm going to pound you right into the ground."

"Thank you."

"Ohhhh, tough talk. Thank you. Think you can go around killing people and get away with it? I'd like to see you try to take one swing at me."

I don't answer.

"You are a stupid little punk."

"Thank you." I try to smile. It takes an hour to wear him down.

Mr. Lester stops and gives me a thumbs-up. "I think you're getting the hang of this. It's not always going to be so easy," he says.

"I know." I will know some of the kids at school, but not all of them. Even the ones I knew before, I don't really know them anymore. I've been gone so long. Going back to school won't be easy.

But it will be easier than Great Oaks.

GREAT OAKS ~~SCHOOL~~ PRISON

My last night at Great Oaks. I gather my papers together. My first list is at the top of my stack…just my name. I walked into this place without a clue.

I put my old lists with my letters. I don't want to read my old stuff. I want to think about the future, about going home.

I climb out of bed and spend the night half awake, half asleep, staring out the window. Before dawn, I see Dad's car in the parking lot. I must have been dozing when he drove up.

The sun has barely come up. Mr. Lester waits on the front steps with me while Dad finishes signing papers in the office. The giant oak trees cast long shadows over the building, but out past the trees, down by the road, the world is beginning to brighten.

"There's something else on your list, you know, and I fully expect you to get it done," says Mr. Lester.

My apology.

"I will," I say. But really, how will he know if I do it or not? I am on my way home.

"I'll be checking up on you," he says, and I wonder if he can read my mind.

I search his face to see if he's joking. He's not.

"Home visits." His voice is serious. "Once a week to start."

Dad comes through the front door. "All set?"

I stand on the steps of Great Oaks School and look up at Mr. Lester.

"See you next Friday," he says. He shakes my hand.

HOME

"Is Mom okay?"

"She's fine. Gonna have that baby any day now."

"Baby Regina," I say, trying to get used to the idea of having a sister. "What are we gonna call here, Gina? Reggie?"

Dad smiles. "Let's get to know her first. We might have to pass on the nickname you had when you were a baby."

"What?" No one ever told me about a nickname.

Dad laughs. "Stinky pants."

"Stinky pants! No way."

"Yes way."

Just like every baby, I guess.

We drive for a while in quiet, and Dad keeps looking over at me real quick and then back at the road. I wonder for the first time if he even trusts me to come home.

Dad clears his throat. "Did you do much running there at Great Oaks?"

"Not much."

"Running, it's still not my thing. But have you noticed I'm in better shape?"

I didn't notice. Who looks at their dad's shape? "Yeah," I say. "Sure." I take a good look at him. He's thinner, and not just a worried, sagging thinner; he may even have a muscle or two.

"I bought some bikes, a mountain bike and a race bike, and I've been riding every day." He clears his throat. "I even ride all the way to the office." He waits a moment. "The truth is, I bought four bikes, two for me and two for you."

"You bought me *two* bikes?"

"I thought we could race together." He shrugs one shoulder. "Or if you only want to run, they have biathlon races, running and biking. We could be a team."

Racing with my dad is something I never thought of before. I nod. "Yeah, Dad. We could be a team."

When I get home, Uncle Grant pulls me down into the basement. I watch him lean to his right every time he lifts his left leg down a step. The first thing I see is my race medals hanging on the wall next to Uncle Grant's.

"Check this out." Uncle Grant moves his arm to the workbench. Elephants, horses, clowns are scattered along the top along with paints, brushes, and bits of fabric.

"Great," I say. But it has been so long. I can't even feel the excitement I had before when I wanted to make a circus in Grantville. I haven't thought of it in forever.

"Cast your eyes over here." I look past Ryan's sign to the grass beside the castle. My tigers are up on a platform—bits of yellow, red, and orange surround their feet. "Ready, set." Uncle Grant flips a switch. Flames shoot into the air around the hoops. "Go!" The tigers jump through the flaming hoops.

Fire. "How did you do it?" I reach out and touch the colored flames.

"It's this really thin thread. I mixed the colors and put a small fan underneath."

"Way cool."

After dinner I walk around River Falls. My room is the same. My house is almost the same except Dad's exercising, Mom has to stay in bed a lot, and Uncle Grant has moved out. The thing that is most different . . . me.

I walk to Red Brick Elementary. I can't resist peering into Ms. Lacey's window. It's just an empty classroom. I lean my head against the glass, close my eyes, and imagine her standing in front of the room. *Breathe, observe the world around you. Be life smart, students, not just school smart.* I can almost hear her singing us through the day.

I walk downtown, past Tiny's Pizza, and stop on a hill overlooking an enormous parking lot. Below me is a huge white-and-gray building with a globe on its roof. Red letters spell out "Sports Tropolis." I sit on the hill and watch. People drift through the doors, cars creep along the parking lot. From above, everything looks like a computer game, like I could click on people and send them back inside, or move my mouse and steer cars. The whole scene feels unreal.

Construction site, gone. Boarded-up comic-book store, gone. Old grocery store, gone. And that's not all. The people below will never know. There should be a sign...something. I now know why people put wooden crosses and flowers by the road instead of at the cemetery—because people pass back and forth on roads.

People walk in and out of doors at Sports Tropolis.

I wish for a can of black spray paint to write "Ryan Was Here" in big black letters. I'd never do it, of course. But I imagine it. I stand and move my hands like a little kid with a sparkler trying to spell a word before the orange lines evaporate in the night.

I can't put it off any longer, the last thing on my list. I turn my back on Sports Tropolis and walk to Howell Street.

HOME

Ryan's grandpa is sitting in his lawn chair on the porch. I freeze at the edge of the sidewalk. He meets my eyes and takes a long drink from his bottle. I walk up the steps that I helped Ryan and Dad build. He's now looking off into the distance. I take a deep breath and ask, "Can I go in?"

He nods and looks down at the bottle. I pull open the squeaky screen door. As soon as the door clicks shut, an old lady calls, "Virginia? Virginia, that you?"

"No." I try to sound confident, but it is all I can do to keep walking. The house is a mess like before, maybe even a little worse. It reeks of garbage and rotten food and cats.

"Virginia!" I follow the voice to a small bedroom at the end of the hall. The floor is covered with blankets and piles of clothes. A long wooden bench is buried under papers. In the center of the room, a tiny lady is propped in the middle of a huge bed.

It is so quiet I can hear her breath rumble in and out. It sounds deep and strong for someone so small and so old.

"Who's there?"

"I'm Robbie. I knew your grandson, Ryan."

"Come here, boy. You talking about my child?"

I step closer. The blankets are drawn up to her chin, showing only her head. The rest of her body is so thin, lost in the wrinkles of the bed.

"Your grandson," I say.

She has a pointy nose and chin, even her cheeks are pointy. Her skin is tight and shiny with hardly any wrinkles. She turns her head to me and looks me up and down.

"I don't know what you want with that daughter of mine. She's had every trouble in the world. I told her not to marry that boy."

"I was talking about your grandson, Ryan."

"He was trouble. Ran around with all kinds of thugs. Criminals even. But she married him. She did. They had a boy, too."

I step closer. A cat springs up and leaps off the bed.

"I went to school with her son, Ryan."

"The boy's dead," she says, still sounding angry at her daughter for getting married. "Got shot. The little one is dead, too. Moved in here with us before he died. He was a good boy. Nothing like his father. A good boy."

We are finally talking about the same thing. I say what I have come there to say. "We got in a fight. We were fighting. It was an accident."

Her eyes are frozen on my face. They're blue with gray flecks. And even though when she speaks her words scatter, I can tell she understands. Her eyes know everything.

I take a shallow breath through my mouth. "I'm sorry. I'm so sorry."

"You're a good boy, too. I can tell. I'm expecting my nurse any minute. I don't have any cookies to offer. But I thank you kindly for your visit."

"Thank you."

Out on the porch, I take a long breath of cool, fresh air. Her husband is slumped in his chair, probably asleep. I stand in front of him and try to force the words out. I move my lips. "I'm sorry," I mouth without really making a sound.

I start down the stairs and he calls out, "Son."

His one word punches my skin. I jump. He stands and walks over to me. "There's some things you just can't change."

"I know and I'm sorry."

He doesn't answer, so I head down the steps. He adds, "And then again, there's other things you can."

"Yes, sir."

It grows dark on my way home and tiny stars are scattered across the sky. They're soft and dim, like they need to warm up to shine properly. One star shines brighter than the rest.

Mom is on the porch swing when I get home. "How're you doing?" I ask.

"I'm fine. Your dad's the one going crazy. He keeps looking at me like 'Is it time?' Does he think I'm going to have this baby and not tell him? He needs to chill."

"I thought of a middle name for Baby Regina."

"Really?" She puts her toes down and stops the swing.

I sit next to her. "What do you think about the name Star?"

"Star." Mom says it slowly, like she's rolling it around in her mouth to taste it. "Regina Star Thompson. It's beautiful, Robbie, just beautiful."

We sit together for a long time, looking up at the sky, my head on her shoulder and her hands on her belly.

"She'll have your same initials." I can tell by the sound of her voice that she is smiling.

"RST," I say.

"I never noticed that before . . . right in a row."

I could tell Mom about RST right now, but I don't want to think about Mr. Michaels. If my sister ends up with old onion breath for a teacher, she won't have anything to worry about. He'll have two RSTs to deal with.

Acknowledgments

I am grateful to the students who read early versions of the manuscript: Alexandria, Samantha, Ciara, Cortney, and Savannah. My heartfelt thanks to the family of Kimberly Colen and the Society of Children's Book Writers and Illustrators for the Kimberly Colen Memorial Grant, and to Laura, Steve, and Cookie Butler for their support of my work. I would also like to thank Professor Byron Steiger, Bill Reiss, Julie Amper, Eleni Beja, Colleen Lippert, Donna and Mike Epley, Kelli DuBois, Linda Gustafson, Elsa Guzman, Ann Talley, Marvin and Karen Terban, Caron Cohen, Kelly Milner Halls, Roxyanne Young, Cynthia Leitich Smith, Verla Kay's blue board, RUCCL, and the following writers: Kathleen Ahrens, Donna Earnhardt, Marta Bliese, Laurie Cutter, Sarah Johnson, Norma Klein, Christina Boland, Theodore Curtis, Shelley Seely, Lindsey Leavitt, Jeanne Lit, PJ Lyons, Sondy Eklund, and Elfriede Moehlenbrock. Most of all, thank you to everyone at Holiday House for bringing Robbie's story to the world.